THE LAST
300
MILES

THE LAST
300
MILES

G. Stewart Nash

CAITLIN PRESS

Published by
Caitlin Press Inc.
Box 2387, Station B
Prince George, BC V2N 2S6

Cover design by Roger Handling, Terra Firma Graphics

Interior book design by Sheila Adams, Eye Design Inc.

Maps designed by Rich Rawlings

Cover images: (back cover)First Bridge at Hagwilget, BC Archives, Call #A-06048; (front cover) Snowshoes, Lenard Sanders, photographer.

National Library of Canada Cataloguing in Publication Data

Nash, G. Stewart, 1942-

  The last three hundred miles

    ISBN 0-920576-90-7
    I. Title.
    PS8577.A72L3 2001   C813'.6   C2001-910809-5
    PR9199.4.N37L3 2001

Caitlin Press Inc. gratefully acknowledges the financial support of the Canada Council for the Arts for our publishing program. Similarly, we acknowledge the support of the Arts Council of British Columbia.

Printed in Canada by Houghton Boston Printers and Lithographers

BRITISH
COLUMBIA
ARTS COUNCIL
Supported by the Province of British Columbia

The Canada Council for the Arts
Le Conseil des Arts du Canada

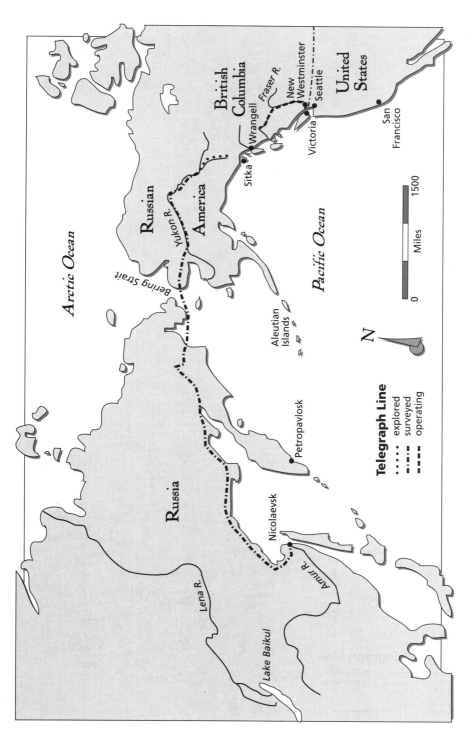

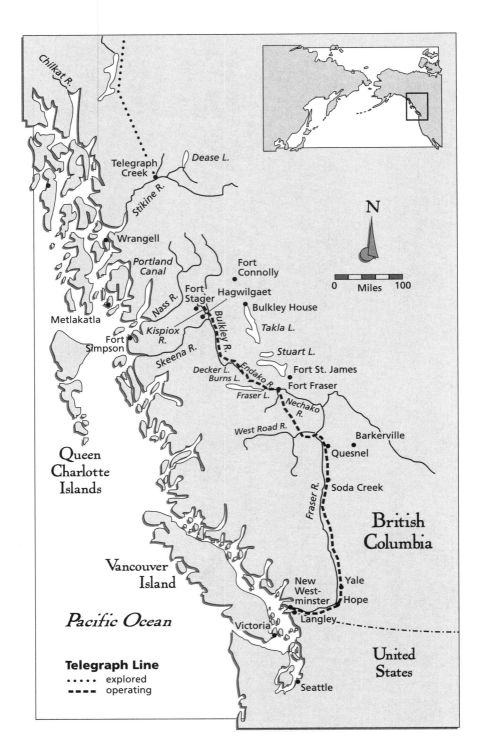

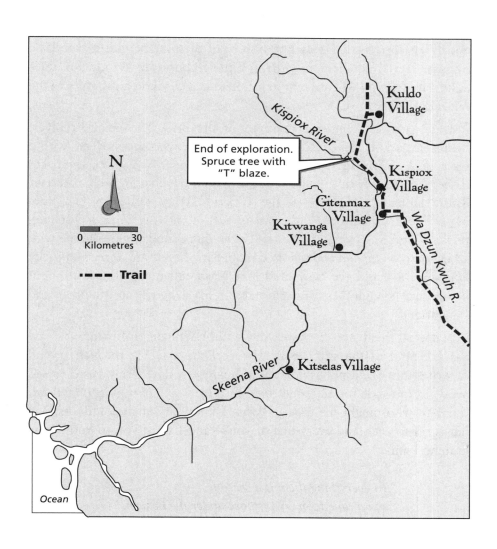

End of exploration. Spruce tree with "T" blaze.

ACKNOWLEDGEMENTS

I WOULD LIKE TO THANK THE FOLLOWING INDIVIDUALS FOR THEIR PERSONAL input, perspectives and suggestions, as well as providing research materials which has revealed a fascinating history of the time period. It would be impossible to list them in order of the importance to me for their contributions, so I will attempt to list them in a chronological order as the novel developed.

Katy Hughes, reference archivist at the B.C. Provincial Archives. Kathleen Larkin, Prince Rupert Public Library, who supplied me with a great deal of information at various times over a two year period. Dr. Robert Galois, whom supplied a lengthy list of possible research materials. Kathy Holland, Librarian at the Gitxsan Treaty Office in Hazelton. My wife Sandy, who patiently put up with numerous hours of listening to the irritable clacking of keys as I sat in our cramped motorhome with a keyboard on my lap and whom critiqued my first draft. Terry and Vicky Hansen, Dave and Lee Nash, and June Nash, all contributing with input in one way or another. Rob Sterney for his expertise in grammar and suggestions.

A special thank you to best-selling author William Hoffman, who saw the potential of the story, patiently working with me through several re-writes to make it publishable. And finally, my dad, Grant, who passed away far too soon for any of us, unable to read my novel in its final draft; the man who taught me most of what I know about the outdoors. My hat is off to each and every one of you — and I want you to know how grateful I am.

> "To everything there is a season,
> and a time to every purpose under the heaven."
>
> *Ecclesiastes 3:1*

PROLOGUE

THE SMALL CREEK RAN THROUGH A DEEP GORGE GOUGED OUT OF the mountainside. It had taken centuries for the water to cut its way through the rocky hillside. Further up the mountain, one of the smaller side channels had cut through a large vein of quartzite, laden with a yellowish natural element fused to the quartz, as if it had been glued there by the finger of God. Men became obsessed with the seeking out and extraction of this element from its natural state. Gold could make a man rich beyond his wildest dreams and it could lead to his end, suddenly, unexpectedly.

At the edge of the stream bed, the sluice box had been set up the day before. This was the first full day working the small gravel bars lying on top of bedrock.

The two prospectors tested the choice gravels with their gold pans after descending into the small canyon. They were pressing northward to Buck's Bar in the far reaches of the Colony of British Columbia, having heard of a huge gold strike there. Both of their pans showed colour with the first washing. Two hours later, they found a small nugget of gold.

They spent the first night on the bluff above the spot where the small gold nugget had been found. Frank Duprey and Roger Arthur hastily made a makeshift camp. The fire had not yet burned down to coals by 11:30 and it had just turned dusk in the far north country. A half moon occasionally showed itself through breaks in the clouds, and the two men had just fallen asleep to the sounds of water rushing along the boulder-strewn creek.

Roger and Frank were suddenly jolted awake by a loud piercing cry: *"Awwwoooo wooo wooo"* sounding out in the nearly dark night. Frank sat upright halfway through the scream. Their minds groped frantically, trying to identify the nearby haunting noise that woke them.

"What in tarnation is that?" Frank whispered to Roger.

"Danged if I know. It ain't no cougar or wolf."

Another cry rang out: *"Haii-haii-haii."* It echoed up the canyon, deeper in tone than the first noise.

"Mother of God," Frank said. "I'm gettin' my gun."

"Shhhh. That other critter will hear ya!"

"Don't care, Roger. That thing knows we're here. Why ya think he's callin' to that othern'?" Frank grabbed his rifle, jacked a cartridge into the chamber, and turned to face the first wild sound.

Another single "*Haiiiiii*" rolled up the canyon. Frank wheeled in that direction, his rifle raised to his shoulder. Seconds later, he spun the other direction to face the first noise again, but saw and heard nothing.

Dawn came at three in the morning. Roger and Frank had built up their campfire for the duration of the night, taking a torch and rifle to gather additional firewood. Their ears strained to detect unusual noises over the sound of the creek below, but none were heard. They spoke little of the two strange screeches until it was totally light.

"Want some breakfast, Frank? Don't think that thing's around here anymore."

"Yeah, guess we might as well. I'm tired as heck, but I can't sleep none. Probably won't tonight neither."

Though their packs were heavy their supplies were limited, and meals were generally skimpy, just enough to keep up their strength. At the Gitanmaax[1] trading post, they'd purchased what they needed for this last leg of the journey. They also traded a couple of knives for smoked salmon at Kuldo Village[2]. For breakfast they had hardtack, coffee and a piece of smoked salmon. As they ate, they talked about the frightful sounds.

"What ya think that animal was last night, Roger? Were the two the same kind of thing, or were they two different critters?"

"I been trying to figure out all night what made those noises. I ain't never heard nothin' like it. I think they were the same, 'cept one's bigger'n the other. And I think it was answerin' that first one, like they were communicatin' or somethin'. Heard porcupines in the night once. Sounds like a woman cryin', but that was sure no porcupine. With a howl like that, I'd say these are big critters…or banshees, or somethin'. I just don't know."

"You think we oughta scout around, see if we can find tracks or somethin'?"

"That's a good idea, Frank. I'd like to know what the heck it was. See if it's still hangin' around here. But I ain't goin' no where's without my rifle. No sir—no where's!"

They finished breakfast, while Roger made lip smacking noises, like always. They grabbed their rifles and scouted the area from which the closer creature had screamed, never more than a few yards apart. Not finding anything: such as moss disturbed the way moose and deer hooves do, rocks turned over by bears, or broken twigs on the ground as if something heavy had stepped on them, they gave up and returned to camp.

Frightened to spend the night in the same location, they moved their possessions across the creek to a small clearing in the trees. Their new camp in shape, they assembled a small sluice box they had designed. If they found enough gold in their sluice, they would cut trees and makeshift a larger one.

Each carried a metal shovel in his pack, minus the handle, along with the head of a pick axe, and they scouted around until they found suitable handles for each of the tools, keeping their rifles close at hand. Once assembled and fastened, the tools adequately fit their needs.

The two prospectors carried the sluice box and tools down into the small canyon, setting up in a likely spot. They worked the pockets behind the bigger boulders at the water's edge, carrying a canvas bag full of gravel to pour through the sluice. They worked through the rest of the day and each time they cleaned out the sluice, they recovered several dollars in gold. It was the most productive area they'd found after several months of testing.

"Frank, we'd better quit for today and git some wood gathered for another all night fire…jist in case."

"You're right. Don't want somethin' scarin' us in the middle of the night again, so I'm wonderin' if we oughta take turns sittin' up and keepin' the fire going. Kinda watch out for somethin' sneakin' around on us."

They cleaned up their sluice and by 8:30 P.M. had $60 in gold. As they hiked back up to camp, they discussed their chances of continuing to find the small productive gold pockets to sluice out. If their luck continued, they could fill their small leather pouches with $800 to $1,000 of gold in two weeks, and still make it to Buck's Bar before winter set in. They could buy a winter's supply of grub in the mining town, and rent a cabin if one was available. But unless they found bigger nuggets soon, this was not the mother lode they'd hoped for the last four years. Perhaps, they thought, they would return and take time to explore further up the mountain, hoping to find the source.

The night passed without incident, both men taking turns on guard duty. The next day proved another good one with the sluice. They worked until 10:00, then picked up the rifle they kept nearby, filled the canvas water bag, and started uphill for camp.

Halfway up, Frank stopped and held up his hand. "Ya hear that," he whispered.

"What? I didn't hear nothin' but the creek."

"Shhh. I thought I heard a *'wooo'* up by camp. Maybe that thing's back."

"Frank, ya been jumpy fer two days now. You're jist trying to hear somethin'. I'd of heard it if it *'woooed'*. Sides, it's still daylight. Don't think it comes around in daylight."

"Well, I'm keepin' my gun ready jist in case. I'll blow its damn head off if it's up there. I ain't takin' no chances."

Frank led out, slower than before. His ears strained to hear another *'wooo'* noise, his eyes darting back and forth through the trees. On occasion, they had to grab a small tree or limb to pull themselves up the steep incline, while their zigzag course helped cut down the steep grade. Frank's head popped up over the top of the canyon, and he stopped, looking up and down the rim, then back through the trees, watching. For what? Some shadow of movement? Some unusual colour? Anything out of the ordinary.

"Come on, Frank. Let's git to camp. I'm tired and I'm hungry. There's nothin' up there."

Frank stepped up onto the rim and stopped again. Roger pressed on past and headed straight for camp, with the canvas water bag swinging from his hand as he stepped over fallen logs. As camp came into view, he thought he saw movement and stopped.

Frank caught up to him. "What?"

"Not sure. Saw somethin' move in camp. You take the lead…and be careful. It might be one of them Indians. Don't be a shootin' nothin' you shouldn't, okay?"

Frank walked ahead slowly. The ground beneath the dense hemlock trees was covered with moss, absorbing noise from their footsteps. Carefully, they stepped over dead tree branches scattered about the forest floor to eliminate any sound of breaking twigs. Their camp sat in a small opening in the midst of the dense timber. They had scraped away the moss around their campfire, down to bare ground, so none of the sparks would smolder and catch fire.

When they could see most of their lean-to shelter through the trees, they stopped and watched for movement. Suddenly, they heard a loud grunt, and the canvas shelter was jerked from its moorings and pulled out of view.

"Geez...ya see that?" Frank said.

Roger stood with a puzzled stare, wondering who or what could have grabbed the canvas shelter and pulled it from the tie downs. It would have taken more than one man to break those ropes like that.

As they stared at the spot where the lean-to had been, a dark form stepped into view and looked directly at them. Both had seen bear stand on their hind legs, but neither had seen one walk on them. This tall creature stood on two legs, as a man would, but this was no human. Its height and bulk were much greater than any man they'd ever seen. Even in the shadows, they could tell it wore no clothes, but was completely covered with hair, and its arms hung down past the knees.

"What the hell is that?" Frank asked, loud enough for the creature to hear.

"Don't know, but it ain't no Indian. Shoot the damn thing."

Frank raised the Joslyn breech-loading .52-caliber rifle to his shoulder and flipped the safety off. The noise from the rifle shot rang through the trees.

The impact of the bullet knocked the creature back a step, and its right arm raised and placed a hand upon the left side of its chest. It looked down at the blood trickling between its fingers.

A second crack from the rifle spun the creature around and it collapsed to the ground, emitting a high-pitched scream. The sound diminished as its life faded.

"I think it's dead, Frank. Ease your way over there and let's make darn sure."

They slowly worked their way to the edge of camp. Their canvas shelter lay in a heap, covering the small rock cairn inside which they'd built their cooking fire.

The fallen creature lay on its side. Frank poked the end of the rifle barrel into the bottom of a foot, but this roused no movement. Its foot was shaped like their own, only much larger. The sole looked like the pad on a dog's foot. Inch long hair hung down alongside the rough pad.

Frank, still holding the barrel of the rifle toward the creature in a defensive posture, moved slowly toward the beast's head. Roger stayed in back of Frank, who prodded it in the thigh, belly, and finally the neck.

"Yea, he's dead fer sure. Got him in the heart both times, I think. Too damn close ta miss. But, geez…what in tarnation is it?"

"Don't know. Haven't seen nothin' like this before. Look at those humongous hands. Just like a man's. Phew, stinks somethin' terrible! Shoot it again…make darn sure it ain't coming back to life, then we can skin it, or somethin'. This thing might make us rich."

"What the heck ya gonna do with a skin, Rog? Pack it clear outta here? That skin probably weighs more than a hunert' pounds."

"Just shoot it, Frank. We'll figure out what to do later on."

Frank pointed the rifle at the beast's temple and pulled the trigger. The impact made the creature flinch, and Frank jumped back a step.

A deafening high-pitched roar arose from behind them. Startled, they whirled to face a second, even larger hairy creature approaching fast. This one was a darker colour, almost black, with silver tipped hair and a large scar on the side of its hairless face.

Neither man moved, frozen with fear. The huge beast swung its left arm in a backhand motion, sending Roger sprawling to the ground.

Frank frantically put another shell in the chamber and started to bring the rifle into shooting position as he turned to face the creature, but the giant reached out and placed a huge hand on the rifle. Towering over him by three feet, it looked down at Frank, who in turn looked up into its eyes. They were a dark reddish colour and Frank sensed the anger now piercing his own eyes. Then it screamed out another different, horrifying sound and Frank noticed dark-coloured, square-shaped worn teeth, and smelled the almost unbearable stench from its mouth. Frank knew he was going to die a horrible death and could do nothing to stop it. He wished now he hadn't shot the other animal.

The creature jerked the rifle from Frank's grip, held it in both hands above his head and gave a quick wrench, snapping the thick wood stock like a twig. In another slower, wrenching move, it bent the barrel into a quarter-moon shape. The iron barrel snapped with a loud pop.

The monster dropped the broken pieces at its feet, grunting softly. Looking at Frank's face again, it placed a hand on the top of his shoulder and began to squeeze slowly. Frank winced from the tremendous pain. His face distorted in agony and his cries changed to "ahhh...ahhhh!" The shoulder bone crushed in the giant's grip, and Frank screamed in excruciating pain just as Roger raised his head, still groggy from the backhand blow.

Roger watched in horror as the beast jerked Frank to its side and placed his head underneath an arm, pressing it against the top of its hip. With the free hand, the creature pushed down on Frank's shoulder; Roger heard the neck bones break, a sickening crunching sound.

He couldn't believe what he saw next as the hairy giant pushed harder on Frank's shoulder, blood gushed out in an explosion. Frank's head and neck had been ripped from his shoulders, and his torso crumbled limply to the ground. The severed head rolled near the fire-pit, and blood seeped onto the canvas lean-to.

The giant directed its attention to Roger. Seeing him still alive, the creature bellowed a loud angry roar and took three quick steps, the third ending on Roger's rib cage.

Roger's cries of, "No...noooo," echoed down the small canyon, drowned out by gurgling water flowing over rocks in the small clear creek below.

The hairy giant returned to the side of its fallen mate and, kneeling alongside, tried to prod it into rising. After several attempts, the giant realized his slain companion would never get up again and wailed in agony over its death. Finally, it picked the dead mate up and with one hand and arm beneath the stomach, carried it off into the dense forest.

CHAPTER 1

IT WAS LATE AFTERNOON APRIL, 1865, WHEN HUGH RANDALL cupped his hands around his mouth and hollered across the brushy draw to Stephen Doyle.

"Okay, that's good right there. Mark it."

Stephen had been holding the survey rod for Hugh to sight on and take his reading. The markings on the rod were in direct correlation to the marks above and below the center cross hairs in his transit telescope. Thus, Hugh could determine the distance to the rod.

Stephen drove the wooden peg in the ground, marking the approximate position for the last boundary corner of the survey. Later, they would measure the distance with a Gunters Chain, and before measuring the corner points more accurately, they would have their client come to the site and approve the corner positions.

Stephen walked down through the brushy draw and up to Hugh, who was placing the survey transit into a wooden box in the back of the buckboard wagon.

Stephen, a slender-hipped, broad-shouldered man of twenty-six with curly, dishwater blond hair and hazel eyes, looked taller than his 6'1". Full of life, he made people laugh at his single sentence quips. He could imitate accents he picked up in the fast-growing city and practiced them when alone until they sounded natural. A likable man, admired by ladies for his looks and humour, he was respected by men who had the opportunity to observe him at his work. He was intelligent, innovative and quick to learn the surveying trade. People expected him to take over Hugh Randall's business when Hugh retired.

Hugh placed the wooden box containing the transit into a larger box padded with old blankets. The rough terrain leading to town would bounce anything in the buckboard to pieces, if not secured.

"Okay, boss, let's hit the trail for home." Stephen climbed onto the buckboard and Hugh clicked twice out of the side of his mouth, slapping the lines against the horse's back. "Rachel said we're having a pork roast for supper tonight. Boy, I love that pork with mashed potatoes and gravy. What are you having for supper?"

"I never did like pork meat. Just give me warm beans with cheese and a slice of bread and I'm set. Since Adell passed away, I don't cook a whole lot, so I'm not particular any more."

Hugh's wife had died of consumption two years after they arrived in San Francisco. She and Hugh were never able to have children, and now at 62 years of age, a widower and childless, he regarded Stephen like a son.

Hugh learned land surveying in Philadelphia over thirty years ago. When he heard stories about California and how fast it was growing, he pulled up stakes in 1850 and brought Adell to San Francisco where he began his own and soon very successful surveying business. After she died, his work became his life. He put in long days and many late nights. The more occupied he kept himself, the less he thought about Adell and how much he missed her. Occasionally, he met ladies who seemed interested in him, but he never pursued the attention they showed, preferring to work or read. He'd always liked reading about others experiences in places he would never get to see. One of his great desires was to travel overseas. Perhaps when he retired, he would think on it seriously.

As Stephen earned Hugh's trust, Hugh gave him more responsibility. Stephen encouraged Hugh to get away from the work, go to a theater, take a weekend trip to a fishing spot, and enjoy different diversions in life. Hugh grunted about it every time, but eventually found himself doing some of what Stephen suggested.

"Well, I'm sorry to hear you don't like pork meat, Hugh. I was about to invite you for supper."

"No, no, thanks anyway. I don't want Rachel going to any trouble for me."

They rounded the corner and started down the street to Stephen's house. He'd invited Hugh for supper on a spur of the moment before, catching Rachel off guard and embarrassing her a bit. Hugh had to clear his throat as they neared the house, as he often did. It used to be a small annoyance to Stephen, but he'd grown to accept it.

Hugh stopped the wagon in front of Stephen's home. "Next Friday evening then, boss?" he asked. "You come to supper and Rachel will have plenty of time to prepare. Is that all right with you?"

Hugh grinned. "Yes, son, that's all right. Tell Rachel and Michael hello for me, and you go ahead and take the weekend off. I'll pick you up next Monday morning, at a quarter to seven."

Stephen opened the door and stepped into a pleasing aroma of roast pork. Michael came running across the floor, arms extended, shouting, "Daddy! Daddy!" and leaped into Stephen's open arms. He was five and a half years old and a daddy's boy. Stephen always romped around with him: wrestling, being a horse, chasing him from room to room. He built his son little farm buildings and carved animals from wood he found out in the hills. Stephen took Michael everywhere he could, carrying him on his shoulders. They were best buddies.

Rachel entered the living room and, as she smiled, the narrow space between her front teeth showed. An attractive woman with brown hair laying softly on her shoulders and three to four inches down her back, she had large dark brown eyes set in an oval-shaped face. Even in her full apron tied around her slender waist, she presented a pleasing sight for Stephen's eyes. They embraced and kissed, a lingering tender kiss that reminded them of this special night of the week, after Michael fell asleep.

"Oh, before I forget, I invited Hugh over for supper next Friday night...ah, if that's all right."

"Certainly it's all right. You should have invited him over tonight. I have plenty."

"Well...I thought about it but remembered that he doesn't like pork, so I thought we might have something different next week. Maybe a nice cut of beef steak, if you can find some at the butcher's."

They had a pleasant meal and, at 9:30, Rachel shook Stephen's shoulder as he sat slouched in the easy chair, snoring softly. When she turned down the wick on the bathroom lamp and came into the bedroom, Stephen was ready for her.

Stephen had come to San Francisco from northern Virginia, near Harrisonburg, at age nineteen with his father, Wilfred, and sister, Eileen. Stephen's father and grandfather had been carpenters, the grandparents emigrating from Ireland when Stephen's father was fifteen.

Stephen had learned the carpentry trade by age twelve, but intended to do something different with his life, to use his quick mind and not spend endless hours at the work bench. He loved the outdoors, often going into the hills carrying his squirrel gun that he bought with money earned helping his father. With it he'd bagged several whitetail deer, and a black bear. Squirrel stew and hot biscuits with honey ranked among his favorite meals. His father hunted too, and most of their meat came from wild game.

In the fourth grade, Stephen came out on the losing end of his first fist fight with the school bully. His father told him that whenever he had a fight he couldn't talk himself out of, he'd better get in the first few blows, startle the opponent and finish it quickly. Stephen grasped the concept, remembered it and put it to good use in grade twelve against a different bully.

He met a surveyor working in Harrisonburg and asked the man for a job. The surveyor talked with him a while and took down his name, impressed with the lad's initiative. The following year he called on Stephen, now seventeen, to help him on a job in Lynchburg. Stephen jumped at the prospect, and against his father's wishes, worked for the surveyor the remainder of the summer, staying away from home three weeks at a time.

At eighteen, Stephen's mother died of a sudden unknown illness and he quit the surveying trade to help his father, who now had a difficult time keeping up with work while trying to cope with caring for Stephen's fourteen-year-old sister and his grief over the loss of his wife. Too many objects and memories reminded him of her. During that winter, Wilfred decided to move from Virginia, the further away the better. That spring they left for St. Louis, where they caught a wagon train bound for California.

Wilfred died in an accident when he fell off a high scaffolding at a new building project in San Francisco two years after they arrived. Stephen and Eileen, now in her last year of school, remained in their father's house. Stephen had been working for Hugh for eighteen months and earned enough to make ends meet when he met Rachel at a dance. They were married a year later, three months after Eileen married the first mate of a clipper ship that freighted along the west coast. He'd moved her to Seattle and Stephen wrote them every few months.

The weekend turned out to be a fun one for Stephen Doyle and family. They rented a small skiff equipped with a sail and made their way across the wide San Francisco Bay toward the north side where they planned to camp on a small sandy beach. As they sailed, Rachel told Stephen some of what she knew about the area in which they lived: how a community called Yerba Buena, or good herb, became San Francisco in 1848 with a population of 800; how it grew to 35,000 within two years after gold was discovered at Sutter's Mill, fostering much lawlessness until a vigilante group numbering 9,000 men restored law and order. She and her family had arrived in 1852 when the vigilantes were active and swift to justice. Many of the worst criminals were hanged. She also told them about the hundreds of ships at the docks bringing in new people and trade goods and leaving with others, some of who were shanghaied and never heard of again.

At the sandy beach, they swam and lay in the sun, fished and hiked in the hills, and were tired out completely when they arrived back home Sunday evening.

The following week proved busy for Stephen and Hugh. They returned to the survey site they were on last Friday, accompanied by their client, who revealed plans for a university his group planned to build.

The surveyors worked on various other jobs throughout the week. Stephen had become proficient with the mathematical calculations required for all their surveys. Square blocks and lots were not a challenge to compute closures and areas for, but irregular shaped parcels needed a number of rigorous mathematical steps. The logarithms book and slide rule became worn from usage.

Hugh had one other employee, Waldro Fraser, who was being trained in land surveying. He and Stephen did most of the harder field work. On occasion they needed extra men to work; axemen, stone-scriber's and chainmen were hired locally when a government contract was obtained to survey out an entire township, thirty-six square miles. Hugh did most of the map drafting, spending much of his time in the office where he could be accessible to the clients.

Late that Friday afternoon, Stephen and Waldro returned to the office. Waldro left for home while Hugh and Stephen discussed the accomplishments in the field that day. At 6:30, they locked up and stepped into the wagon. A chill glazed breeze wafted out of the west, and they glimpsed a fog bank covering the harbour as they rounded the corner at the top of the hill. From a distance they heard fog horns from three different steamships echoing off the bay and through the streets as they trotted the horse toward Stephen's home, in anticipation of a nice beef steak dinner.

"Stephen, take the lines while I button up my coat. It's a darn cool breeze for this time of year."

"Aye…yer jist gittin' old, mate," Stephen answered in an English seaman's accent. "Afta put an extra warm brick in yer bed tonight. *Har har har!*"

Hugh looked ahead, a smile spreading across his face. He enjoyed Stephen's different accents and brogues.

Stephen stopped the wagon in front of his house. "I don't see a light in the living room…not even one coming from the kitchen. I was sure the lamps had plenty of oil in them last night."

He swung down off the wagon and tied the horse to the single hitching post. "Maybe we ran out of matches or something. Come on in and we'll see what the problem is."

As Stephen opened the door, he hollered, "Hellooo in there. How come it's so dark?"

No reply. Michael did not come running across the living room floor to jump into his arms. Stephen expected them to shout out, *"Surprise!"* as they had on his last birthday. But it wasn't his birthday, and no shout of surprise greeted him.

"Wait here, Hugh," he said, feeling his way in the dark interior. "I'll get into the kitchen and light the lantern. See what the heck is going on here."

Stephen lit the lantern on the kitchen table. There were no dinner place settings. He felt the wood stove. Barely warm. He opened a lid on top and saw only glowing coals remained. He turned toward the living room as Hugh stepped into the kitchen.

"What's wrong, Stephen? Where are Rachel and Michael?"

"I don't know. There's no note on the table. Let me check the living room."

He took another match from the wooden box and lit the living room lamp. Seeing no note, he carried the lamp to the upstairs bedrooms and found everything in place, except for a couple of wooden toys by Michael's bed.

Returning to the kitchen where Hugh sat at the table, Stephen said, "I've no idea where they might be. They've always been here when I come home. They're never out at dark unless I'm with them." He stared at the floor. "Something's wrong here, Hugh. What should we do?"

"Anywhere she would have gone today…shopping for dinner perhaps?"

"Yes! She would have gone to the butcher shop, for sure. Probably the market also. That's a good idea, Hugh. Let's see if they're still open… see if Rachel still might be there, or least walking along the street."

Not finding either shop open or seeing them along the way, Hugh suggested they go to the police station. Once there, Stephen ran inside and explained the concern for his missing family.

"Mr. Randall," the man at the desk said, "there was an accident this afternoon and it involved a lady and a child. You should go to the hospital right away. It could be them." Stephen's face paled. Starting toward the door, a nauseous feeling swept over him. He staggered outside, not wanting to believe it could be his Rachel and little Michael. He quickly told Hugh what he'd heard, grabbed hold of the lines, shouted at the horse and cracked the whip on its rump repeatedly as they raced to the hospital. Hugh clung to the side of the wagon in fear for his life. He'd never run his horse this fast, but kept the concern to himself.

Stephen leaped from the wagon and raced up the concrete steps, taking three at a time. He flung open the door just as Hugh's foot touched the ground by the wagon. At the front desk, Stephen asked frantically, "My wife …my wife and baby…are they here? The police said they might be here!"

The desk nurse responded, "I'm sorry, sir, who is it you're looking for?"

"My wife! I'm looking for my wife, Rachel…Rachel Doyle and our son Michael. He's four." He held his hand out just below his waist to show her how tall he is.

The nurse's expression quickly changed to one of compassion as she thought of the dead child and the injured young woman who had been run over by a loaded freight wagon. "Please wait here a moment, sir. I'll get the doctor for you."

"You mean they're here?" he said, as a sinking feeling swept over him.

"Please just wait a moment," the nurse said, then hurried along.

Hugh came through the door while Stephen paced back and forth in front of the large nurses' counter; thoughts racing through his mind, like bees entering and exiting their hive. The door at the end of the hall opened, and a tall, older man dressed in a buttoned long white coat with two noticeable blood stains, walked slowly toward him.

"I'm Doctor Lessard. The nurse tells me you are looking for your wife and child."

"Yes, yes, I am. They weren't at home. Are they here? Have my wife and son been in an accident? The police said…"

"Please follow me. But I must tell you before we go back there, that this may or may not be your loved ones. You will have to identify them. The child died at the scene. The mother has just passed away. We worked frantically to save her, but there was just too much damage."

A wave of nausea swept over Stephen as he imagined his wife and baby Michael being dead. "No…it can't be them," he said as he looked away. "It just can't be!"

The doctor gently held Stephen's arm and led him into the operating room where a nurse was cleaning up. They approached a narrow flat table where a heavy white cloth covered a woman's body. Stephen stopped alongside the table, not wanting to see the face beneath the cloth. The doctor moved to the opposite side of the table and asked Stephen to step closer. Stephen's knees weakened and sweat beads gathered on his forehead. As the doctor reached for the cover, Stephen held his breath. His adrenaline surged when Dr. Lessard began to remove the cloth covering from the head. Suddenly, time shifted, as if the doctor's movements were happening in slow motion.

Seeing the hair first, he recognized it as the same colour as Rachel's and as the cloth moved further down, he saw the forehead and closed eyes. "Oh, no! *God, no. Not my Rachel.*" The thought leaping across his mind like a bolt of lightning. He closed his eyes and fought the lump building in his throat, but tears clouded his vision when he opened them. Partially focusing, he saw her full face, and let out his breath. The adrenaline stopped as quickly as it had come.

It wasn't Rachel.

CHAPTER 2

S TEPHEN AND HUGH WERE BAFFLED REGARDING THE WHEREABOUTS of Rachel and Michael. They returned to the house in hopes the two were there, but found no one. They went to several neighbors and two of Rachel's closest friends. No one had seen them. The last place they thought of looking was Rachel's parents' but they were not there.

The three men discussed what they should do, then Rachel's father followed Hugh and Stephen back to Stephen's house. He'd assured his wife they would find Rachel, and everything would be fine. On the way, they stopped at the police station once again to report the disappearance and were advised that first thing in the morning, descriptions would be distributed to other police stations around the city. The three men separated, searching the city streets the entire night, hollering out Rachel's name, not concerned about waking up sleeping people.

The following day, one lead had put Rachel and Michael at a rough part of town near the wharf, but the police investigation as well as numerous inquiries by Stephen and Rachel's father, led only to dead ends.

Stephen took a full month off work, questioning everyone he could, showing their wedding photo. His father had told him many times, "If you're going to start a job, then give it everything you have to finish it," and that advice became part of Stephen's nature. For five months, Stephen continued searching for Rachel and Michael whenever he was not at work. He began to search less and less, running out of places to look and ask questions.

The humour had gone from Stephen's character and he grew disheartened. He returned each night to a cold, lonely house. He kept all Rachel and Michael's personal things just as he had found them that night in hopes that somehow they would return.

Now it was Hugh who admonished Stephen for not getting out and doing something more with his life. "Come fishing with me this weekend, son. The steelhead are running up the Sacramento River. Nothing like fighting a feisty fifteen-pound rainbow trout on the end of your line." That grabbed Stephen's attention. He had never caught a fish of that size before.

The weekend found the two on a small passenger boat to San Pablo Bay and then renting a guide with a skiff to take them through Carquinez Strait and into the Sacramento River where they fished for steelhead. They caught two apiece the first afternoon and cooked one of them over an open fire at the evening camp.

Their guide had spent time in the northern part of the California gold-fields between 1850 and '52. He told Stephen and Hugh stories of the claim jumpers he encountered and the fights that broke out in saloons, mostly over dancing girls and cards. He told them of the few who found a large enough gold nugget or a single pocket of small nuggets that grub staked them for more than a year. And he also told them of a giant hairy man-beast a few of the miners claimed to have seen in the forests.

"What do you mean, a hairy man-beast?" Stephen said. "There's no such thing."

"Sonny, I'm just tellin' you what those miners told me. If you'd a been there to see them tell it, you'd a swore they were sayin' the truth. They were scared just to tell it. Said it must've been eight–or nine-feet tall. Had kind of a reddish brown hair all over its body. Stunk somethin' terrible, they say. Walked on two legs just like a man. Even the Injuns have legends about it up in northern Californi'. I think there's somethin' there all right, sonny, hidden in them deep woods."

Stephen chuckled at the thought. "I'll tell you what, pardner, you can believe that BS if you want, but I would have to see one standing right in front of me before I would believe it!" He snickered again at the picture forming in his mind.

They caught additional fish the next day but the guide acted indifferently toward Stephen who sensed that he had inadvertently called the man a liar, but was unsure how to make amends. When leaving the guide, Stephen offered him two of the largest fish he'd caught, and said, "Sorry about last night, pardner. No offense was meant."

The guide looked at Stephen, then spoke in a hateful tone. "I hope you do see one of them giants face to face, sonny. I hope he scares the living hell outta ya!"

The survey work slowed somewhat during the cooler winter months, and heavy rains plagued the Bay area. Early spring saw numerous rain showers also, but by June the warmer weather and sunny days brought many survey jobs to their doorstep. The news of the surrender of General Lee at Appomattox ending the long civil war in early April, sang out along the tightly stretched telegraph wires crossing the continent and seemed immediately to spur the economy. But for a brief period everything came to a standstill when the same telegraph wires that had carried good news to San Francisco, also carried shocking news. On April 15, President Abraham Lincoln was assassinated.

Stephen had been slowly regaining his humour and returning to what Hugh called "almost a normal human being again."

It was late in the afternoon on June 21 when Hugh sat Stephen down in his office. "Stephen, I need to talk to you about something very important, something that will take some deep thought on your part."

"Sure, boss. What's on your mind?"

"I've been contacted by Charles Bulkley of the Western Union Extension Company here in 'Frisco. They're constructing a telegraph line up through the Colony of British Columbia, then across a short stretch of ocean to hook up to a line in Russia, and then into lower Europe. It's called the Collins Overland Telegraph, and they are racing against time; racing against that cable they're trying to lay across the Atlantic Ocean. The first one to hook up to Europe will be the major communication supplier, so it will be very lucrative for them.

"There's a three hundred mile stretch remaining to be explored, and a survey map made. They're needing a surveyor to complete it in the fastest time possible. The line crew may be starting on that stretch before winter sets in. Bulkley contacted me to see if I could help. I assured him I was not up to the task but that I had a competent man who might be interested. I told him I would talk to you about it. It would be quite an adventure. What do you think?"

Stephen sat in silence. He couldn't see himself in a foreign country mapping a telegraph line.

Hugh tilted his head, looking over the top of his eye glasses at Stephen's blank stare. "Stephen," he said to break the silence of the moment.

"There is no way I can do that!"

"Son," Hugh said softly, "you are very capable of conducting that kind of survey. You have basically been doing the same thing for our clients from time to time. The only difference is the type of terrain you have here, or had back in Virginia, as compared to what's in British Columbia; more trees, fewer people, not many trails, different biting insects, and maybe a bear or two. So, why do you think you couldn't do it?"

"Well, I can't leave you strapped with all this work and besides…"

Hugh held up a hand. "Waldro and I can handle the work. We'll just need to train someone to help Waldro in the field. What else?"

Stephen shuffled in his chair. "Hugh, I don't know anything about that country. The only exploring I've done was working with you out in the mountains or taking off with a squirrel rifle in Virginia, but I was back home every night, or back at camp."

"There has never been an explorer, son, who knew much about the country he was exploring. That's the excitement about undertaking a grand task such as this. You would only be gone a few months and, no, you wouldn't be able to return to a warm bed every night, but you would experience something very few people in the world ever have. It's a great opportunity for you, Stephen. Your name would be entered in the history books if the telegraph line is successful. If I were up to it, we would both go."

Rachel and Michael infused his mind. "I just can't go, Hugh. What if my wife and son come back? If I'm not here for them, they…they may leave again."

Hugh hadn't spoken to Stephen about his missing family for several months. He rose from the chair and walked to Stephen's side, placed a hand on his shoulder, cleared his throat, and picked his words carefully.

"Son…Rachel and Michael did not just decide to disappear of their own accord and then, perhaps, come back to you when they are ready. Had that been the case, she surely would've been in touch with her own parents by now, don't you think? She wasn't the kind of woman who would just up and leave her home and husband on a whim. As far as I know, you never had troubles in the marriage. And if I'm right about that, I'm probably right about the other. So you need to face the fact, son, that they have been missing now for over a year, and outside of some miracle, they are never coming back. You have to move on with your life, Stephen. Your family would tell you the same thing." Then Hugh remembered that Stephen didn't have a family except for his sister in Seattle. He felt badly for having said it.

Stephen sat in silence. Hugh had become his mentor, not only in surveying but in business and financial matters as well. Stephen's thoughts weighed heavily and Hugh felt compassion.

Finally, he broke the silence. "I tell you these things because I care about you, Stephen. But it's been a long day and we're both needing to relax. Come, let me take you to dinner tonight. I know you must have a hundred questions about that wild country. I'd bet you'll take right to it, just like you did that steelhead fishing."

Back in Philadelphia, Hugh had read the published journals of a surveyor named David Thompson who'd explored a portion of western Canada in 1811. On the way to dinner he was telling Stephen what he remembered about the country up north and suddenly recalled a paragraph that Thomson had written concerning a strange set of tracks in deep snow that appeared like huge human footprints, fourteen inches long and eight wide, with no shoes and four plainly visible toes. Hugh said that it reminded him of that fishing guide's description of a giant hairy man-beast. Stephen shook his head, snorting at the thought.

After Stephen's first drink, he began questioning Hugh about the possibility of having his name go down in history. They discussed various aspects of the possible journey through dinner and up to Stephen's door step.

At 4:15 a.m., sleeping soundly, Stephen suddenly sat upright in fear. He'd had a nightmare as never before, with such intensity that he couldn't believe it only a dream. A giant hairy creature that stood upright on two legs like a man had run across the small meadow with such speed, Stephen hadn't time to raise his squirrel gun. Its huge hand reached for Stephen's face when his body jerked to escape the terrifying moment.

He couldn't get back to sleep that night. The vision of the giant reminded him of what the fishing guide had said and their parting words, the guide hoping Stephen would come face to face with a giant hairy man-beast. The dream alone had accomplished that. Stephen consoled himself; no creature like that existed.

Two days passed before Stephen made the final decision regarding the telegraph project. He wrestled with the thought of closing his home and what Rachel would do if she returned. His mind teetered back and forth, one minute telling him he should go, and the next, one more excuse why he shouldn't. He also feared he might not gather all the right information on the exploratory survey. What if his evaluation and information were not adequate for a decision that apparently would be made as soon as his results were known? Knowing that he just might enter the history books in a small way bolstered his ego. Yet he had a fear of failure tugging at his emotions and his pride.

At the end of the second day, he told Hugh, "I've made up my mind. I'm pretty sure I want to go on that telegraph job."

Hugh pushed his chair back, and looked at Stephen in a somewhat disappointed manner. "Stephen, my boy, you cannot be pretty sure about going on an adventure such as this. You're going to go and get the job done, or you're going to stay here and learn about someone else doing it. No more wishy-washy stuff! They need to know right away. So you tell me what it's going to be. Are you going to do it, or not?"

Stephen took a deep breath, puffing out his chest more than usual, and said in a Scottish accent, "Ya got the right man for the job, laddie. Point me the way north."

"You big horse's rump. It's about time you started coming around. I'll set up an appointment with Mr. Bulkley tomorrow. You better make arrangements for your house. He may want you to leave within the week."

The following day, Stephen walked into Charles Bulkley's office at the Western Union Extension Company. He'd never seen an office so large and elaborately decorated. Bulkley's desk, three times the size of Hugh's, was made of dark cherry wood with a glass-covered top. The two chairs in front of the desk were covered with rich dark coloured leather, and high-backed with arms of oak—the ends carved in the shapes of lions' heads. The back of the chair Bulkley sat in towered more than three feet above his head. Cigar smoke filled the room.

Bulkley said, "Mr. Doyle, you've agreed to undertake a job that requires the kind of skills that Hugh Randall tells me you have. He gave me your background and assured me that you are a man of honesty and integrity and would see a job through to the end. Is there anything you wish to add to that assessment?"

"No, sir," he said with confidence.

"Good." Bulkley slid back into the chair and took a deep draw from his cigar, blowing the smoke upward. "My man, Edward Conway, is in charge of the telegraph line—everything, including route exploration and survey, moving of materials, the actual line construction and telegraphers at station offices. It's a monstrous job and he has done it well. You'll meet him at his office in the British Colony capital city, New Westminster. He'll assign your duties there."

Bulkley took another puff on the cigar. "I would bet you have a lot of questions, and I know right now, I won't be able to answer them all. I'll do what I can, though."

"How long will I be up there and what will I be paid for the job?"

Well, Mr. Doyle, how long it will take to find us a route is up to you. We have about three hundred unexplored miles, as the crow flies. That doesn't mean you're going up there and walk the whole distance to Buck's Bar and back and be done. Conway tells me he thinks it's going to be rugged tree-covered country with several river crossings to contend with. Those are not little rivers up there. You'll be taking a steamer up one of them, nearly to your starting point. Had it built up at Puget Sound by Seattle, just for those swift rivers. We named it the *Mumford*.

"I would guess you'll be up there three or four months. We will furnish all of your needs: food, equipment, trading goods and all the supplies needed for the north country this time of year. And extra cash to carry with you for additional purchases. You better take warm clothes. I'm told winter can come overnight up there. As for the money, we guarantee you fifteen hundred dollars at the completion of your survey and with a letter of requisition from Mr. Conway. How does that sound, Mr. Doyle?"

'Fifteen hundred dollars,' Stephen whistled under his breath. That's more than he made by working for Hugh all year. This wouldn't be so hard, he thought, the money blinding him to the rugged terrain Bulkley warned about.

"Yeah, that sounds fine, Mr. Bulkley. I'll do a good job for you, sir. When do I leave?"

Bulkley grinned at the young man's sudden enthusiasm. "Our company steamer, the *George S. Wright*, will be leaving with a load of supplies and equipment in six days. You'll need to purchase all your supplies and have them at the dock for loading by 6:00 a.m. The freighter will stop for an extra day in Seattle for a few things we're making there, including a type of harness to help set up the poles. Our new ship, *Mumford*, will leave there the same day as the Wright, and transfer of supplies will occur on the Fraser River at New Westminster. You'll board the *Mumford* for the trip to your drop-off point on the Skeena River at a Indian village called, Gitanmaax. At least we trust the ship can make it that far. No one's tried it before but we've one of the best Captains' around. Any other questions you can think of, Doyle?"

"No sir, Mr. Bulkley. I can't think of any. I know I'll have several before I get a block away though."

Bulkley laughed heartily as he stood and said, "Yes I know you will too, Doyle. Now let me walk you downstairs to our accounting office. I'll instruct them to give you a letter of credit to purchase your supplies. But, oh, before I do, let me write down the name and address of a man I think you should go see before you do any purchasing. He's been in the BC Colony, doing some exploring for us. Poor fellow lost a leg up there."

Bulkley wrote down the name Javier Vega. His address was only eight blocks from Stephen's home. Stephen stepped out of the office and into the thrill of a new adventure.

CHAPTER 3

A T MID-AFTERNOON THE FOLLOWING DAY, STEPHEN KNOCKED ON the door of Javier Vega's home. The house looked much older than his own, the outside covered with weathered lumber. The perimeter had a variety of neatly arranged, colourful flowers. Tall rose bushes stood at each front corner of the house. Large pink petals had spread open, the sweet smell permeating the still summer air. "Must be a woman living here." Stephen thought.

As the door opened slowly, an attractive young woman wearing a plain white blouse and light brown skirt stood before him. Sunlight glistened upon the long black hair that flowed down past her waist, to hang upon her hips. Stephen stood motionless and silent, captivated. He looked directly into her deep, dark brown eyes, then to the cheekbones and lips. He'd never seen a woman so beautiful. "A woman most definitely does live here," he thought.

"May I help you, Señor?" she said with a Californio', or Spanish accent, and a pleasing smile.

"Ahh...well...yes I think so," he stammered. "Is this the home of Mr. Javier Vega, ma'am, er...ah Señora, or ah...Señorita?" She giggled at the awkwardness of her language, and Stephen smiled apologetically. "It is Señorita," she said, bowing her head slightly, "And yes, this is the home of mi padre, Javier."

"Is Mr. Vega at home?" Stephen said slowly, emphasizing the words.

She smiled again at his clumsiness. "Yes, Señor, he is at home and I understand English very well."

"Oh," he said, "I...I ahh..." and both gave a chuckle as they looked at each other.

"Please come in," she said, extending her arm. "Who may I say is calling?"

"My name is Stephen Doyle. I've been sent by Mr. Charles Bulkley."

An eyebrow lifted slightly as she recognized the name. "I see. I'll tell my father you're here. Please sit on the sofa, Mr. Doyle. I'll return shortly."

Looking around the living room at the meager furniture, he noticed how clean and neat everything was kept. There were no pictures on the walls, only a wood carving of Mother Mary with a rosary hanging from an extended hand.

The sofa was made from one inch willow and the two cushions were covered with a colourful blanket. Stephen placed a hand on the bare arm to test its sturdiness and with a strong grip gave a pull. Releasing the grip he noticed dirt under his fingernails. He disliked that and quickly began picking at the dark coloured grit, not wanting anyone to see them this way. When the young woman returned he brushed his pants off as he stood, then followed her to the back yard where her father rested.

He watched her walk, noticing how square her shoulders were and especially how well she carried herself, like a lady of stature would. He also watched the twitch in her skirt, suggesting her hips were full and curvaceous.

He'd had no strong desires of lying with another woman since Rachael disappeared. Now, for the first time, being held in a warm embrace flooded his thoughts. He felt guilty, yet he couldn't take his eyes off her. They had walked to the rear of the yard before he clearly saw a man lying on a cot beneath a small shade tree. A rolled-up pant leg pinned just above the knee made the missing leg obvious. A crutch lay on the ground beside the cot. The man finished the paragraph of the book held in his hands and sat upright, swinging his leg to the ground. He too spoke with a Californio' accent, causing Stephen to listen with more attention than usual.

"Mister Bulkley sent you, did he? How is he? Well?"

"Yes, Mr. Vega, he is quite well."

"What was your name again, sir?"

"Stephen Doyle."

"Please sit here on the cot in the shade and tell me why Mr. Bulkley has sent you here." As Stephen sat, Vega added, "Did you meet my daughter, Mr. Doyle?"

Stephen looked into her dark eyes again. "No sir, not formally. She didn't tell me her name."

Vega noticed their locked eyes and the shy smile on his daughter's face.

"Then I better introduce you. This is Mariana, Mr. Doyle. She is my only child. Her mother, Leena, is shopping at the moment and will return shortly. Mariana helps the family by working at the Chinese laundry most days. Mariana, would you bring Mr. Doyle a cool drink while we talk?"

Stephen watched her walk back into the house, then turned to Vega.

"She *is* very beautiful, Mr. Doyle. She is also very particular about men. Many have called on her but none have captured her interest. I've never seen her smile at a man as she has done with you. Are you married, sir?"

"Ahh...I ah..." he stammered. "Well, actually, I don't know, Mr. Vega."

Vega frowned. How can a man not know if he is married? Mariana stepped out the back door with two glasses of water and walked toward them.

"I don't understand, Mr. Doyle. Have you a wife?"

Mariana stopped near the two and waited anxiously for the response.

"My wife..." Stephen hesitated, and Mariana's heart sank as she heard it. "A year ago my wife and little boy Michael went shopping. The butcher sold her meat for dinner. He watched her leave the shop and turn toward the market, but no one at the market saw her. I haven't seen them since that day, Mr. Vega. I searched the entire city every day for a month ...and I'm still searching. I'm in a terrible kind of limbo."

"I understand, Mr. Doyle. If I were in your place, I'm not sure how I would answer that question either."

Mariana's heart went out to Stephen. "I'm very sorry for you, Mr. Doyle. I sense you loved them very much, and still do. It must be difficult for you."

"Thank you, Mariana. Your words are comforting to hear."

Her smile was different, warm and understanding, causing Stephen to imagine stepping into her arms. He wondered what it would be like to be held again.

Perhaps she sensed his thoughts, handing the glass toward him, and the other to Javier. They drank deeply; the cool water soothing their parched throats.

"Tell me, Mr. Doyle, why did Mr. Bulkley send you to see me?"

Mariana sat on the ground with an arm on her father's knee, looking up at Stephen while he told them why he had come. "So I hope, Mr. Vega, that you would be kind enough to tell me something about the country I'm going into and what supplies I need to take."

Just then, Leena Vega came through the back door and, seeing a strange man sitting with her husband, returned through the doorway.

"Why don't you go help your mama, my pretty one?" He said to Mariana, stroking her black hair. She arose, reluctantly leaving the two men.

Vega told him that he hadn't been in the same area as Stephen would be going. They were constructing the telegraph line in the upper Fraser River Valley, near the town of Quesnel. It was near there that he'd been badly mauled by a grizzly sow while searching for a telegraph route, just like Stephen would be doing.

"I was walking around a small knoll covered with blueberries when I heard rustling in the brush above me. I stopped, trying to see what made the noise. A grizzly cub stood on its hind legs, and when it saw me it got scared and started bawling. The sow was uphill a little further and she stood up...and up...and up! Big one she was. Wanted to see what scared her baby. Looked directly at me, then dropped down, running at me so fast I couldn't think. My shot bounced off her sloped skull. She ran right into me, knocking me flat to the ground, biting my head first and then down to my leg. Tore it up real bad. My partner heard the shot and came running. He shot it from ten feet away, right in the ear. If he hadn't been there, I'd be dead. My leg became infected. By the time they got me to a doctor, he had to take it off. When I returned to San Francisco, Mr. Bulkley met me at the boat. He sends me money every few months to help out. He's been kind to us."

Vega advised Stephen to pack as light as possible, and he would often have to subsist off the land. Vega made him aware of the different animals, plants and berries available to eat. Vega recommended a good rain slicker and waterproof tarp to sleep under. The mountains had frequent rain storms, sometimes lasting for weeks.

"Take one of the new 56-caliber carbine rifles with you," Vega said "You may need to get off a second shot to save your life. Ask Bulkley for a partner. No man should go into those mountains alone. Something happens...it's the last anyone will hear of you."

Stephen wrote on a small tablet as Vega talked, not wanting to forget anything. "Take trade items along. The Indians can help you, and guide you to places it might take months to find on your own. They've lived in that country for hundreds of years. No one knows it better. Be their friend…and they'll be yours."

Mariana returned, asking if they would like more water and if Mr. Doyle would join them for supper.

She had told her mother about their guest with excitement in her voice. Leena suggested she ask the gentleman to supper. Delighted, Mariana kissed her on the cheek before heading out the back door with the water.

She had never heard a man with such an unusual deep, yet soft voice, which made her comfortable. Only twenty-three, living in a semi-isolated part of the city, she hadn't much opportunity to meet a variety of people. Fortunately, Javier had been determined to give her some formal education. She and a skinny boy were the only two of her kind to attend an English school at a time when most schools did not allow the Californios.

When she was fifteen, men began to notice her, staring as she walked, and began calling at the house when she was seventeen. Most were gentlemen, but not all. Her parents had made certain she was never totally alone with a man. Not that they didn't trust their daughter, but they knew what dwelt on most men's minds and, besides, it was proper custom.

Mariana was mature for her age, though some thought her childish or bashful because she didn't have a man calling on her regularly. She ignored remarks made by some of the older women, particularly those her own age who had two or three children. She knew one day a man would stand out from the others and would be the first to be invited for supper.

Stephen stared at her beautiful dark eyes once again as she gave the invitation. He immediately accepted. "It would be an honor to have supper with you and your family." Then looked at Javier to be certain he didn't object.

The dinner consisted of food Stephen was unaccustomed to—thinly sliced, spicy, marinated beef, a reddish-coloured spicy rice, refried beans and warm tortillas. The spices were tolerable, but the bite he took from a small green pepper stiffened him before he even had chewed the little devil. Javier broke into a wide grin, seeing how fast Stephen spat the pepper back onto his fork. Mariana apologized for not warning him, suggesting he eat some salt to relieve the burning.

After dinner, Javier and Stephen sat in the small living room and were soon joined by the women. The parents found a reason to excuse themselves from the room, leaving Mariana alone with a man for the first time.

Mariana spoke first. "Your new work in northern British Columbia will be dangerous. It was for my father."

"Yes, I've heard stories about black bears attacking people, but that was the first about a grizzly bear. Other than bears, though, I don't think there's much danger. I'll just need to be careful not to break a leg or some dumb thing like that."

She didn't reply, but thought he might be taking the wild lands of the north far too lightly.

"Mariana, would you mind calling me Stephen? Mr. Doyle sounds too formal and, besides...when a wee laddie talks with a fair lassie, he's ta hopin' she knows his first name." Mariana looked at him strangely, then giggled, realizing he was joking by using the strange accent.

They talked until Stephen noticed the parents preparing for bed. He jumped up and apologized, not realizing how long he'd stayed.

Stephen said "I just wanted to ask...ah, would you mind if I see you again before I leave. It would..."

"No, Stephen, I wouldn't mind. I would like to see you again." He did not hear her door close as he turned up the street and started for home.

In bed that night, he thought of Rachel lying beside him. He had nearly forgotten her touch, her smell, the little things she said to him as they made love. He ached for her many nights, longing to feel her next to him. Now unexpectedly someone else stirred those emotions, differently than Rachel had, and he wanted to pursue the feelings. But guilt weighed heavily. Stephen lay awake much of the night, unable to stop thinking of Mariana, and of Rachel.

Over the next few days he purchased needed supplies. Hugh advised Stephen on which light-weight survey equipment to take and gave him some of his own to use. He also agreed to check on Stephen's house each day on his way home.

Two men sat at a table near the rear wall of a waterfront saloon. One wore a heavy buckskin jacket and a dark brown handlebar moustache, the other a tweed coat and black derby hat.

Carl Hamilton, the man with the derby, was known within the Atlantic Cable Company as a man who accomplished things. He was unerring in details, nothing passed him unnoticed. He'd been ordered to travel from New York to San Francisco to learn as much as possible about the competition, the Western Union Extension Company, whose bookkeeper could easily be persuaded to pass on information for money. When Hamilton heard of the company hiring a local man to explore the last three hundred miles, he conceived a plan to delay line construction, giving the Atlantic Cable Company the advantage.

"What I want to hire you to do, Mr. Evers," Hamilton said to the man in buckskin, "is dispose of a certain gentleman. I've been informed you have the qualities I'm looking for. Is my information correct?"

"Could be...if the price is right. What do you have in mind?"

"There's a telegraph company constructing a line to cross over to Europe, and they have just hired a surveyor to travel to the northern part of the Colony of British Columbia. He's to explore for a route for three hundred miles and deliver his results to them. It's imperative he doesn't complete that exploration."

"That's no problem. I can take care of it right away. Where does he live?"

"No, Evers, that's not how it's to be carried out. I don't want another explorer taking his place. Therefore, it has to be done after he's begun his exploration. When he fails to present his findings, winter will have arrived and that should delay their efforts."

"So, you want the deed done up north where no one will know what happened. What are you willing to pay?"

"How much would you think adequate?"

Evers didn't like being put on the defensive this way. Hamilton might be willing to pay a lot more for a murder if he played his cards right. He searched frantically for a good answer...or a good question that would put him back in control.

"This seems pretty important to you, and I've got a reputation for doing away with men who get in the way—make it look like an accident. That's why my name come up when you asked around. So, I'm not going to sit here and haggle over a price. You already know what you're willing to pay, and if it's enough, you got yourself a man. Just spit it out."

Hamilton hoped to get the job done for less than authorized, planning to pocket the balance. Perhaps he still could, he thought. "I've budgeted $1,000 to the task. Half to be paid before you leave, the balance when you bring me his survey tools as proof.

Evers was surprised by the amount offered. He would have done it for $500. He rubbed his chin as if in deep thought, then finally said, "Okay, if that's the best you can offer then."

Hamilton breathed easier, knowing exactly how he'd spend the extra $500. He informed Evers of the details: when the company's steamer would leave, how he could obtain passage, what the name of the surveyor was, where and when he would receive the first of the two payments, the last one to be paid when he returned with the surveying tools.

Two days before leaving, Stephen arrived at the Vega home and invited Mariana for a walk. Parting, they kissed briefly at the doorstep.

Final preparations were made the following day. He checked and rechecked his equipment, provisions, rifle, ammunition, clothing and trade goods.

At 3:00 that afternoon, Stephen invited Mariana to dinner at one of the finer restaurants, the Comstock on Sutter Street. He hired a carriage and picked her up at six.

"Am I dressed all right, Stephen?" she asked worriedly after his speechless stare. "I didn't know where we were going. In fact," she said, blushing slightly, "I've never been to a nice restaurant. My people are not always welcome."

"Mariana, you look perfect. There's no place I wouldn't take you and be proud to have you on my arm."

Her heart melted. "Will you take me to Canada?" she said, not believing what she had asked. She lowered her head and began to blush.

Stephen too, was totally surprised at the question. "I...I..." he managed.

"No, don't answer," she said, putting her hand to his lips, "I was being foolish. I'm sorry." She smiled and said, "I'm ready to eat, *mi caballero*."

On the carriage ride home, he placed an arm around her shoulders. She slid closer. At the door, he bent to kiss her; and she moved even closer, putting her arms around his neck, pressing her warm lips against his own. After the second longer kiss, she pulled back to see his eyes in the darkness. "Please be careful. I'll be worrying for you."

"I'll be careful, Mariana." Then he added in a deep southern accent, "No need to worry, little lady. Got me a lucky rabbit's foot to carry along."

She didn't smile or laugh at this, responding seriously, "Come back to me, Stephen. I'll be waiting."

Touched, he pulled her close and held her tightly, whispering, "I'll be back, Mariana." After a final lingering kiss, she held his hand until the last possible moment.

Hugh pulled the wagon to a stop at the single hitching post at 5:00 a.m. While Stephen locked up, Hugh struggled to lift Stephen's eighty-pound backpack onto the wagon and had second thoughts about the recurring desire to be going with Stephen.

On the way to the docks they talked about supplies, making certain there would be nothing more to purchase in Seattle or New Westminster. Hugh reminded him of the great adventure he was undertaking and that he should do his best to obtain results for the telegraph company as quickly as possible. Winning this race to Europe would be worth countless dollars. Stephen felt confident he would accomplish the task.

At the pier before boarding the *George S. Wright*, Hugh pulled Stephen toward him and gave him a fatherly hug, telling him to be careful and come back home with his name in the history books. Stephen carried his supplies to the top of the ramp where the first mate held a boarding list, asking his name, company position and port of departure.

"Stephen Doyle is the name. I'm a surveyor and will be changing to the *Mumford* at New Westminister. Then on up north."

He was instructed to board, and told where his cabin would be found. Stepping onto the ship, he walked a short distance along the rail to wave goodbye to Hugh. He barely noticed the man in the heavy buckskin jacket, standing within earshot of each boarding passenger.

CHAPTER 4

THE STEAMER DEPARTED AT 7:00 A.M. BEFORE LEAVING THE LARGE
bay it steamed past an island containing the U.S. Army Disciplinary
Barracks, causing Stephen to wonder what misdeeds a man would have to
do to end up there. In later years, the island would be known as Alcatraz.

Beyond the island and under the mile-long Golden Gate, they entered
the choppy waters of the Pacific Ocean. Stephen remained above deck
until they were well away from the coast, steaming northward. Never having
been on a ship in the wide open seas before, he found it exhilarating. He
moved to the front of the ship, leaning over the rail, watching the
white-capped waves push away from the bow. Walking to the rear of the
ship, he marveled at how far back he could see the ship's trail. The sea air
smelled fresh here, unlike the rotting smell at the docks and along the
shore at the north side of the Bay he visited with Rachel and Michael a
year ago. He wondered if he would have been asked to do this job if his
wife and child were still with him, and if he would have taken it.

The ship ran at thirteen knots, making almost fifteen miles each hour.
It had twin smoke stacks seventy feet above deck, belching black smoke
with sparks blowing off into the ocean. Strapped securely to the main deck
were supplies for the telegraph line: large coils of wire, wooden barrels of
insulators, brackets and daily food rations packed in wood boxes. Stephen
asked a ship's mate how many rations were being transported to the north
country, and there were more than 30,000 individual meals. He began
to realize the immensity of the telegraph construction and the untold
miscellaneous items that supported it.

His small cabin and its bunk left little room for his backpack. At dinner
he sat with five other men at one of the rectangular tables. Overhearing
their conversation, it appeared that four of them knew each other. Stephen
and the fifth man across the table remained quiet through most of the
meal, talking only as they finished. The two walked to the
top deck and looked at the expanse of stars. They remarked on the dim
light on the distant shore which disappeared occasionally, speculating it
represented a farm house among the trees.

Stephen couldn't sleep; the constant droning of the ship's engines, coupled with excitement, caused him to twist about in the old blankets.

The following day he wrote a short letter to Mariana, telling her how fond he was of her and how his words couldn't express how much he enjoyed the time they spent together. He finished by telling her of his guilty feelings regarding Rachel, of his thoughts that Rachel might return someday and of his concern that it would be better if she looked for someone more dependable than he. It was difficult to write these words. He believed he was not entitled to the affection of another woman until he knew what happened to Rachel.

Stephen felt disheartened for the remainder of the trip to Seattle where he would mail the letter to Mariana. The ship docked at 8:15 the following evening.

With a day's layover in Seattle, Stephen got directions from a man working on the docks, climbed the steep dirt street leading away from the wharf and found his way to the home of his sister, Eileen, to whom he'd wired a message prior to leaving San Francisco. He spent the day visiting with her and her two children, the husband being out to sea. The visit lifted his spirits. Eileen helped, talking of old times and gave comforting words concerning the loss of his family.

Before he boarded the ship, Stephen visited a saloon near the wharf. known as one who didn't drink much, he stopped more out of curiosity about the rugged reputation of wharf saloons. Dimly lit, the inside had a putrefied smell from spilled drinks on the wooden floor and reeking smoke. When his eyes adjusted to the light, he noticed the tables were occupied only by men. He had seen very few women around Seattle and wondered if a shortage existed. He discovered later that men outnumbered women three to one.

The bartender didn't notice Stephen. He stood with one leg lifted and the foot placed on a stool, in deep conversation with a man wearing a captain's uniform.

"Could I get a glass of whiskey, sir?" Stephen asked, interrupting the two men. They looked at Stephen as if he'd committed a grave discourtesy. The annoyed bartender spoke roughly. "What is it you want, buddy?"

Stephen reordered the whiskey and the bartender turned to get a bottle and glass while the captain continued glaring at Stephen. His eyes went down to Stephen's boots, then back up again slowly, settling on his face. The man spoke, slurring his words. "Inshabordnate! Oughta' be whipped." Stephen glanced st him briefly, then turned away.

Sipping from the glass and wincing at the burn slowly working its way down his throat, Stephen noticed three of the men—Ben, Sean and Ross — he'd sat with at the dinner table the first night on the ship. One of them waved his hand in an invitation to join them. Surprised at the gesture, Stephen complied. The fourth man seated wore a heavy buckskin jacket, and Stephen vaguely remembered seeing him on the ship.

Stephen took a sip of whiskey, scrunching his face as it burnt his throat again.

"*Yeehaa!*" the man named Ben shouted. "You ain't much of a whiskey drinker, pardner. Hey, barkeep, bring us another bottle over here. We're gonna teach this boy how to drink whiskey!" Ben laughed as he slapped Stephen on the arm.

Stephen declined the offer, but Ben persisted. "Might be the last chance to spend with some fine whiskey drinking teachers. Right, men?" he said, winking at his two friends.

"I'm gonna do my drinking in better company," the fourth man said, glaring at Stephen, then stood up and walked away.

"What the heck you do to him?" Ben asked.

"Darned if I know," Stephen answered. "Don't even know the man."

"Probably never see him again," Ben replied. "Just forget him."

The bartender brought a bottle of whiskey and plopped it on the table. The three friends each pulled out a silver dollar and slammed them down, keeping them covered. Stephen realized they were chipping in for the bottle and laid his silver dollar on the table. The three lifted their hands to look at their coins, then covered them again.

"I've got a tail," Ben said.

"Me too,"

"Well I'll be danged. Another tail!"

Straight-faced, Ben said, "Sorry pardner, you lose. Odd man buys the bottle.

We're gonna teach you a lot tonight." Again, Ben slapped his arm and burst into hardy laughter, and Ross and Sean joined in.

Stephen noticed that Sean stretched his neck forward quite often, as if from an involuntary twitch. It proved to be a slight annoyance and Stephen wanted to ask him about it, but didn't want to embarrass the man.

The four men talked about the new ship *Mumford* and the amount of supplies it would be carrying.

"See that captain setting at the end of the bar over there," Ben said to Stephen. "He's the captain of the *George S. Wright*. Meanest man that ever sailed a ship. None of the crew likes him. Disciplines with a whip, I hear. Don't be getting on his bad side."

"I think I already did." He raised his glass in a salute to the captain, downing the contents.

At 3:00 a.m. the four stumbled back to the ship, the three friends taking turns holding Stephen between them. He threw up twice before finally finding his bunk.

On awakening, Stephen felt dizzy and his mouth tasted terrible. He could still smell whiskey and smoke, the smells clinging to his clothes. He cleaned himself up and washed his teeth several times with baking soda to get the taste and smell from his mouth, then walked unsteadily to the main deck just as the ship pulled into the Fraser River. Forty-five minutes later, they docked at New Westminster. The *Mumford* had sailed ahead of them, arriving three hours earlier. Stephen watched as they prepared to unload their cargo and transfer it to the *Mumford*.

On the dock, Stephen asked a constable where he might find a room for the night near the Western Union Extension Company. The constable directed him to a room and a diner, advising him to stay away from the saloons along the river. Numerous robberies and two murders had occurred recently.

Stephen had no desire to see another saloon. He was still feeling the effects of the previous night.

He walked only a short distance uphill toward the rooms, the fully-loaded wood-frame pack hanging on his back slowing the pace. As he stepped past the end of a building, a sudden hard jerk on the pack sent him sprawling to the ground. Two men attempted to wrestle away the pack, pulling a strap off the top arm. He pushed his shoulder closer to the ground, preventing them from removing the second strap.

"Kick him in the head," one said in a guttural voice.

Stephen moved his free arm to protect his face. The impact was hard and a pain shot through his arm. Then the man kicked again and Stephen grabbed out at the man's foot and caught the heel, causing him to lose balance. He fell backwards as Stephen held on tight.

Stephen pulled the shoulder free of the pack and began to rise, but a painful jerk on his hair pulled him back. Stephen saw the kicker get up and knew he had to act quickly. What his father had told him popped into his mind. "Get in the first few blows, startle the opponent and finish it quickly."

He spun to one side and brought a foot beneath himself, then sprang forwards, vaulting over the pack toward the hair puller. His head drove into the man's stomach, slamming him into the brick wall with an audible *"Oooff!"* The attacker's knees bent slowly, and he slid down the wall.

Stephen quickly turned toward the first man to see him pushing himself up. He leaped over the pack and gave a powerful kick, his heavy jackboot catching the man's jaw. The man crumbled face first to the ground.

He turned back to the hair puller to see him stagger away from the wall. He stepped over the pack and grabbed the man's hair, flinging his head backwards, driving it into solid brick. The man slowly slumped to the side.

Stephen shouldered his pack, looked at the would-be thieves, and said, "Not this time fellers. Not this time."

He found the rooms and examined his arm that took the kicks, finding it puffy and tender. At the diner he ate only a light meal, his stomach churning from the affects of the whiskey and retching from the night before. He returned to his room and made the first expedition entry in his journal.

At 9:00 a.m., Stephen entered the Western Union office where he met Edward Conway, a tall man with wire-frame glasses. They studied a large, roughly detailed map of British Columbia showing the constructed telegraph route. It followed the Fraser River to Quesnel, continued north to Fort George, then west to Fort Fraser, next to a large lake.

Conway explained other company explorers' efforts to find a route beyond Fort Fraser, one party wintering in a hastily built cabin.

The company had finally settled on a route which continued westward to the Wa Dzun Kwuh River[3], because there were better supply routes on the Skeena[4], Nass[5], and Stikine[6] Rivers.

"I've sent two other surveyors to explore a route northwest of Gitanmaax, at the junction of the Wa Dzun Kwuh and the Skeena," Conway said "but haven't heard from them. This is where you come in. I need you to explore northward from here," Conway pointed a finger to the map, "a few miles above a village called Kispiox. I want you to travel up the Skeena, make your way over to the Nass, then down to Buck's Bar, on the Stikine River. It's the last three hundred miles we need to explore. I've made you a small map of the area, but it's a bit crude. The information came from a couple of natives and from final entries of the previous surveyor. What I need from you is an accurate map of a proposed route, with prominent features based on astronomic observations. We need details of river crossings, canyons, rock slides, soil types, timber species and sizes. Anything you see that's pertinent to our making a decision for a route. Do you have any questions, Mr. Doyle?"

Stephen had stayed attentive to Conway's explanation, writing out his instructions before saying, "I understand you have a man to accompany me?"

"Yes, I do. He's one of the men who helped with the route we're working on now. Jock Dubois is his name. He speaks a bit of the native language and is a good man in the bush. He'll meet you on the *Mumford* tomorrow.

The two men discussed the upcoming journey further, Conway asking how Bulkley had hired him and what his experience entailed. Afterward, Stephen felt comfortable enough to ask a question he'd been wondering about since Hugh had mentioned it.

"I'm told the telegraph company who gets their line to Europe first will probably profit untold amounts from it. Is that true?"

Conway seemed surprised at the question, having not really thought about that aspect of the project, concentrating his efforts on getting the line built to the Bering Straits. He thought for a moment, then said, "You know, I have never heard a figure from Bulkley on just what the line would mean to them in a monetary value, but once it's operable, I could see the line busy almost 24 hours a day. The time difference between here and Europe would see to that. Let's say a message went across every five minutes," he said lifting his head, mentally calculating. "That's twelve messages an hour, or two hundred eighty-eight messages every day. At just a silver dollar a message that's two hundred and eighty-eight dollars or," he scribbled on a sheet of paper. "Yes, that's over a hundred thousand dollars a year," and nodded with a satisfied look. "I'd say that's a pretty good profit the first year of operation!"

Stephen whistled and said, "You bet it is. I'd have to work all my life to make that much money. I think we're making history here, Mr. Conway. I surely do." Conway nodded in agreement and they each entertained their own thoughts for a moment. Stephen departed with a handshake and a good luck wish. Closing the office door on July 2, 1866, Stephen felt prepared for whatever the north country had in store.

CHAPTER 5

THE FOLLOWING MORNING, STEPHEN CAUGHT A YAWL AT THE DOCK along with two other men boarding the *Mumford*. Uncommonly, the ship was not docked but had been anchored next to the *George S. Wright* out in the Fraser River.

The Wright captain's life had been threatened by town's people on the dock after he severely whipped a man in front of the ship's crew. A constable was summoned to the disturbance, telling the captain that sort of discipline would not be allowed at a Colony port, and for his own safety he should pull the gangplank and leave. Supplies were being transferred out in the river rather than at the docks where it normally took place.

After Stephen received his cabin assignment, a man near the boarding ladder asked if he was Doyle. It was Jock Dubois, the man who would accompany him through the upper reaches of the Skeena River and over the two watershed divides to Buck's Bar.

Dubois was a short, stocky man with curly brown locks of hair sticking out from beneath his red knit cap. He had a short handlebar moustache, and a French accent. His teeth were stained from tobacco wads held in his cheek.

"So, you are the mapper man from down in the big city that Bulkley sent up, eh?" Dubois said with a grin. "I hope you know how to survive in this kind of mountains, Monsieur Doyle." He gestured toward the mountains to the north. "I am not accustomed to leading a man about like a calf, eh. But do not fear, I will watch over you, for the good of the company." At this he broke into robust laughter, slapping Stephen's shoulder.

Stephen didn't know how to take the remarks. Dubois either thought he knew nothing of the outdoors or had tried to make a joke.

"Jock, let me stow my things and get settled. I'll meet you here in an hour. We'll be spending a lot of time together, so I think we should get better acquainted, discuss our trip and all."

"Yes, Monsieur. We will do this."

"And call me Stephen. I'll feel a lot more comfortable with that."

When the two men met, they talked as the steamer made its way down the Fraser River and headed north up the Strait of Georgia. Parting company, Stephen walked to the front of the ship to watch the conifer-covered islands slip by, like undiscovered jewels floating on the water. He marveled at the height of the rugged mountains far inland and the number of fir trees clinging to steep hillsides. He caught a glimpse of a whale as it rolled the surface, a quarter of a mile from the ship. The shark-like fin on its back and the black and white colouring distinguished it as an orca.

Absorbed by the scenery, Stephen slipped below only twice — once to relieve himself and the second to grab a bite of food in the mess, where he caught a glimpse of Ben, Sean and Ross. He knew he would see them later, so he ate quickly and hurried back topside, staying on deck until darkness overcame the new sights.

Stephen awakened at 6:00 a.m. and could not hear the drone of the steam engine. He dressed and hurried topside, only to see the ship docked. Asking a deck hand as to their location, he learned they were at Fort Rupert on the north end of Vancouver Island, taking on additional coal for fuel.

Watching the men load the coal, he noticed Ben and his two friends working as crewmen. He returned to the cabin and prepared to shave, but thought of the difficulty and necessity of shaving every day on the trail, so decided against it, then went to the mess hall for breakfast. Little of the food appeared appetizing, so Stephen ate sparingly and returned topside, then departed the ship to walk around Fort Rupert and stretch his legs. After returning to the ship, he waited near the gangplank and called Ben to the side.

"You son-of-a-gun. I've never felt so awful before!"

Ben burst into laughter. "You sure tied one on, pardner. Had a heck of a time getting you back to the ship. I think you been whiskey broke now, so you know what your limit is. Come on down and have supper with us tonight, pardner. A few more days and we'll not see hide nor hair of you again. About 6:30."

"Yeah, sure. I'll meet you tonight then."

Taking on the last load of coal, the *Mumford* departed and continued northward, making its way out into the Queen Charlotte Straits.

Near the end of the following day, the ship had consumed most of the coal fuel, due to the heavy load it carried. Captain Coffin laid anchor in a small inlet and ordered the crew to lower the small boats, paddle ashore and cut firewood. By midnight, the crew had loaded enough wood to travel another day. At 4:30 a.m. it began to rain.

The ship raised anchor at 6:00 a.m. and started across Milbanke Sound. The rain continued throughout the day, and as they steamed well into the inside passage, the Captain anchored early to have more wood cut. Stephen volunteered to help, working alongside Ben and his two friends. As the last load was being hauled to the small boats, an eerie high-pitched *"Aaawhaaaaaa!"* rang out from where the dry trees had been cut, startling the wood haulers. Even some of the men on the ship heard the strange noise echoing across the water.

"Holy hell, what was that?" Ben asked.

"Danged if I know," his friend Russ answered. "I ain't never heard nothin' like it. Any of you guys know what makes a noise like that?"

"Not me," Sean said, shaking his head. The other two crewmen shook their heads. They looked at Stephen.

"Not me either," he said. "That's no animal I've ever heard."

"Well, it sure in heck is no wolf," Ben said. "It ain't no bear or mountain lion neither. I've heard all them before. It's strange. It's real strange."

"We got no gun," Russ said anxiously. "Let's get this wood loaded and get outta here before it comes this way."

No one hesitated, quickly moving the cut wood into the two boats and pushing off toward the waiting ship.

"Aaawhaaaaaaaaaa!" the hollow high pitched scream resounded again before they had paddled halfway to the ship. They ceased paddling while the sound ebbed and looked back toward the shore.

"Geeez," Ben said. "That is one strange animal. Let's get to the ship."

The oars dipped faster as they narrowed the distance; the crew glancing often toward the shore.

As Stephen climbed aboard, Jock Dubois was leaning against the railing, looking toward shore. "Jock, did you hear that strange sound from shore?"

"Yes, I heard it. You know what it is?"

"No. I was hoping you might."

"I heard something like that before, eh, the last time I was up north, almost to the Skeena River. We had an Indian guide and two packers with us. He called it Katamnkniest — Man of the Mountain. One of the others called it Bukwas — giant, hairy, wild man — a devil that carried off women and children and ate them, eh. We saw his track. Big! Twice as big as your foot, Monsieur. Must be twice as big as you are, eh?" he said with a toothy grin.

Stephen snorted, disbelieving, while trying to picture a wild man twice his own size. He smiled at the thought, shaking his head.

"It may be true, Monsieur. No other animal makes a sound like Bukwas, eh. The natives have seen him many times. They say he is an outcast from an ancient tribe. It is best that we do not laugh at what they know."

Stephen looked at him a moment. "I need to get out of these wet clothes. I'll see you later, Jock."

He considered what Jock said as he walked to the cabin, thinking it strange to hear of two mythical creatures within a few months. A giant hairy man and a giant wild devil that ate Indian children. He wondered how these legends got started.

Stephen joined Ben, Sean and Russ at the mess hall. The meal served the third night consisted of the same items as the two nights before—salt horse and salt pork. Stephen hoped this would be the last of these meats, but had an uneasy feeling there would be more coming.

They talked about the strange screaming sound they'd heard, and Stephen related what Jock told him. The three laughed at the idea.

Stephen saw the man wearing the heavy buckskin jacket enter the mess hall. He watched him curiously, as he filled his tray and sat with two other men across the room. He wondered why the man had been rude at the bar and wondered where he was headed, and for what purpose. He didn't believe him a company man: he never worked as a crewman. Likely he was just a passenger headed north. A few more days and it wouldn't matter, as Stephen would be getting off the ship far up the Skeena, and the man would stay onboard headed to his own destination.

The next day while anchored to gather wood for the boilers, Captain

Coffin spotted a deer close to shore. A moment later a rifle shot rang across the water and the deer staggered and fell. The Captain hollered toward the small boat starting back and told them to bring the meat back to the ship. The Captain had it taken directly to the cook for the evening dinner.

The crew and passengers were quite pleased with the change from salt pork and horse, except for one man who wouldn't taste a morsel of the wild game. Venison, he said, is no food for a white man. Stephen enjoyed the taste immensely; it brought back memories of deer hunting in Virginia.

At the north end of a channel, the sternwheeler *Mumford* turned inland toward muddy water, beginning the ascent up the Skeena River. Forty miles further, the ship met the full force of the current at the head of tidewater. Working its way into the mainstream of the high swollen waters, it became obvious that Edward Conway's prediction had been correct. Conway had warned Stephen he might be hiking up the river. The higher company officials did not heed his advice to build the ship for strong river currents, and it now looked doubtful it could push through this swift rain swollen water.

Captain Coffin tied up to the bank and ordered half the supplies unloaded. A rough warehouse was built to stow the cargo.

A second attempt brought the steamer further upstream, where it encountered a larger riffle in the main channel. Crewmen in the boiler room threw everything they could into the furnaces. The ship shuddered under the strain, then suddenly began to float backwards. The captain ordered the anchor dropped, and the ship tied fast.

The supply commander, James Butler, met with Captain Coffin and they decided to hire a fleet of canoes and Indians from Fort Simpson to freight the supplies upriver. Captain Butler took a few men in a lifeboat and went downriver, then thirty miles north along the coast to the Hudson Bay trading post. He returned with a fleet of large wooden canoes, the largest having a dead weight of two tons. The group of natives brought their canoes alongside where they were loaded with as many supplies as each could carry.

Captain Butler instructed Stephen and Jock to load their gear in a canoe and travel upstream with this first trip. Ben, Sean and a young man named Charles Morison were among the crew selected to accompany the natives to help unload, build a shelter, and store the supplies.

The Indians looked upon the Skeena as one of the most dangerous rivers to travel by canoe. Only a few had the skill to be trusted with steering.

Freighting up the Skeena in a heavy-laden canoe proved extremely hard work. They were propelled by means of poles, and more often by tracking from the shore with a long rope. The river's width varied greatly depending on the particular area. In places where the centuries of flow eroded through igneous or shale rock, the width was generally two to three hundred feet. But where the water flow slowed and numerous giant cottonwood trees towered over the banks, the river widened to five and six hundred feet. The men took advantage of the many side channels formed by islands as it became necessary to cross and re-cross the main channel several times a day.

The *Mumford* returned to New Westminster for more supplies while the fleet of canoes worked their way upriver. Suddenly, the group of Fort Simpson Indians stopped and began unloading the canoes. They had been discussing the onerous trip amongst themselves and were thinking that no man had enough money to pay what they'd agreed on. They didn't believe they would be paid adequately for the amount of work they were doing, so returned down the river, highly irritated at the white men.

When he could, Morison made entries into a personal journal, writing beneath his rain slicker. After supplies were stored in a makeshift shelter, Morison stayed behind as guard while Butler and the crew returned to hire other canoes. After a good luck handshake from Ben and a wave to Morison, Stephen and Jock began their trek upriver.

The two men followed a well-worn Indian trail that a native in their canoe had told them about. The trail proved slippery wherever sodden earth was not rock covered, making travel slow. Rain began to seep through their slickers. They used treated double canvas covers over their heavy backpacks, in hopes of keeping their supplies and extra clothing dry, but most items became damp from humidity.

Searching for a suitable campsite near a clearer side stream, they came to one at 7:30. They strung up their lean-to shelter and cut the ends of pine boughs to put beneath their bed rolls. As their tent was just large enough for the two, their packs were left outside in the open, covered with an extra tarpaulin. Dubois could see Stephen had woodsman skills and campsite knowledge, but not the way he was accustomed to. Coupled with Stephen's complaints about the rain, Jock knew it would be a long two months.

They were packed and ready to leave camp at 6:30 a.m. Stephen led out, seventy feet ahead of Jock, when a rifle shot shattered the soft pelting sound of rain falling on the leaves. Startled, he whirled to see what Dubois shot at and saw Jock's body smash to the ground, face first, the weight of his heavy pack making the impact harsh.

His first thought was that Jock's rifle had fired accidentally. A second shot cracked the air and the bullet smashed into a tree behind Stephen. His heart leaped to his throat, realizing someone had almost blown his head off. From the far side of their camp, he heard another cartridge being worked into the chamber.

With an urgency for survival, he dove to the side, landing in tall brush amongst the trees. The tops of the willows swayed, giving the marksman a possible target. The next crack of the rifle cut a willow branch, which fell on Stephen's legs.

He wrestled the pack off his shoulders and groped for his rifle, finding it beneath the pack. It took two jerks to free it from the weight, and he had difficulty manoeuvering the rifle into position, the barrel getting caught in the thick brush. Willow tops swayed as he worked it free, giving the appearance of a wounded man thrashing about or trying to escape, causing the mysterious shooter to move forward quickly. Stephen worked the rifle free and jerked his body around, lying flat on his back in time to see a man's leg and rifle barrel emerging past a tree, only a few feet away.

When the man's shoulder came into view, Stephen fired from the awkward position. The large bullet from his .56-caliber Sharps ripped through the edge of the tree, splattering bark and wood splinters. The bullet, mushroomed and slowed by the impact with the tree, struck the man's shoulder. He fell backwards against another tree, the impact knocking the wind from him and as he slumped to the ground, he fell to one side, clinging to his rifle. His dark brown felt hat rolled off to the side.

Stephen scrambled to his feet, jacked another round into the chamber and stepped forward cautiously, keeping the barrel trained on the middle of the heavy buckskin jacket. He tilted the man's head with his boot toe, wanting to be certain of the face and dark brown handlebar moustache. The jacket didn't fail his memory; it was the same man who had refused to shake hands in the Seattle saloon.

Stephen grabbed the rifle from the man's hand and, seeing a knife, pulled it from its sheaf and threw it toward his pack. He was unsure where he'd shot the man. He could see no blood.

Stephen wondered, why had the man tried to kill him? "Why did you shoot Jock?," he said, and turned to see him lying face down in the mud.

He rushed back to see Jock's head soaked in blood, mingling with rain water. He leaned the rifles against a tree and, bending down, rolled Jock's body onto its side, the heavy pack on his back stopping it from rolling further. Jock's forehead had a large gaping hole, with shattered pieces of skull bone and skin clinging to the outside edges. He'd been shot in the back of the head, the bullet entering just above the bottom of his red knit cap. He hadn't felt a thing; dead before he hit the ground.

The rain mixed with blood flowing from the wound, and Stephen almost retched as pieces of Jock's brain trickled down his forehead and onto the ground. He couldn't believe Jock dead, having spoke to him only moments ago. "You lead today, Monsieur," Jock had said. "It is your lucky day! No?"

He reflected on the prophetic words. Had Jock led out, he would be the one lying in the rain with his brains blown out. He wanted to thank God for sparing his life, but was uncertain how to do so with his partner lying here, dead.

Grabbing his rifle, Stephen walked determinedly toward the killer, hearing a groan as he approached. The man struggled to sit up, crying out in pain when he put weight on the shoulder.

Stephen pointed the rifle at his chest and shouted, "Why did you kill my partner?"

The man grimaced, rocking his head back and forth, as if to relieve the pain.

Stephen poked the rifle barrel into the man's shoulder. "Hey," he repeated with more authority, "I'm talking to you…why did you shoot my partner?" The man remained silent. Stephen rammed the barrel harder, shouting, "Hey!" even louder.

"Leave me alone."

"Leave you alone?" Stephen said, his anger growing. "You just blew my partner's brains out and barely missed me. Now you're laying here crying like a baby and you want me to leave you alone. I oughta put a bullet in your fat head, you rotten bastard! If you want to live any longer mister, you'd better start talking." He jabbed the barrel into the man's ribs for emphasis.

"Wait, wait," the killer said, lifting an arm as if to stop him. "I think my shoulder is shattered and I hurt like hell. I'll tell you if you give me a chance. Just don't get trigger happy." His head fell to the ground in pain.

"Start talking then!"

"I was hired to keep you from finding a route for the telegraph line. If I got rid of you, no one would know until you didn't show up to give a report."

"Why's that worth two men's lives? What's so important about it? Who hired you to do this?"

"A man in San Francisco. Paid half down to bring your survey equipment back. Said it would delay the telegraph line."

Stephen thought the man's answer made sense. If he didn't get the information to Conway, the work on the telegraph line construction would be delayed several months and could cause them to lose out to the company laying cable across the ocean. He wondered if they were behind this. "Was the man who hired you with the Atlantic Cable Company?"

"Don't know. He never told me."

"How did you get up the river? You didn't come with the supply canoes."

"I followed the canoes upriver on an Indian trail to where that Morison guy guarded the stuff. He said you weren't too far ahead. I told him I was ordered by the captain to help you guys with your survey work."

Stephen turned away in disgust and walked to his pack in the willows. Hearing the man cry out in pain again, Stephen looked in time to see him struggling to pull a pistol from a holster beneath his bottom leg. Stephen rushed forward, grabbing the arm just as the pistol was raised. The gun fired, missing Stephen by inches. They wrestled briefly and the man released his grip, the shoulder pain proving too great.

Stephen stood, wondering if the killer had any other weapons hidden. He checked him carefully to be certain. Satisfied, he looked at the pistol and debated if he should throw it to the side or keep it. It was a Smith and

Wesson .32-caliber six-shot with rimfire cartridges, and a five-inch barrel. He shoved it into his belt, picked up his rifle and laid it near his pack. Pulling a piece of rope from the pack, he sat the man upright and tied him to the tree, then returned to Jock.

He gently removed Jock's pack. Having no shovel to dig a grave, he didn't want to leave him in the woods to be eaten by wild animals. What could he do, he wondered. Jock had told Stephen he'd married a widow with two children and lived near Fort Langley, not far from New Westminster.

After going through Jock's pockets and pack, retrieving personal items he thought should be returned to his wife, he'd decided how best to dispose of his dead partner. Struggling to shoulder the limp body, he felt relieved Jock weighed no heavier than 140 pounds and carried him to the Skeena River less than two hundred yards away. He wrapped a length of rope from Jock's pack around a large rounded river boulder, then tied it to Jock's waist. He said a short prayer, then hesitantly pushed the awkward bundle into the river. The boulder rolled only a short distance and stopped, and the body floated near the surface. He prepared to wade in and push the boulder free. Suddenly, the heavy rock shifted and rolled slowly across the bottom, boulder against boulder. Jock's body slipped beneath the surface, into the depths of the river.

Stephen placed Jock's pack to the side of the trail behind a tree. He kept some food items for himself and leaned Jock's rifle against the pack, thinking he might retrieve it when he returned. Looking over the murderer's rifle, he grabbed it by the barrel and slung it as far as he could into the brush.

Stephen returned to the man in the buckskin jacket, wondering what to do with him. He'd noticed the shoulder wound when he'd tied him to the tree and now bent down to examine it, but couldn't get a clear view unless he untied the rope. Doing so, he squatted in front of the killer and pulled the buckskin jacket back over the shoulder, followed by his shirt. The skin was split wide from the impact of the large mushroomed bullet that tore through the edge of the tree. When the bullet hit the collar bone, it had shattered it, and Stephen had a clear view. There was no exit wound out of the back.

"You'll live, buster, so I'm taking you back to Morison's camp. When the men return upriver with the rest of the supplies, they can take you back to New Westminster — to hang, I hope." Stephen recalled the name he'd given in the Seattle saloon. " Max is your name, right? What's the rest of it?"

Max was the name he'd chosen to use when he bought passage on the *George S. Wright* at San Francisco. The man hesitated to answer the question, thinking of his circumstance, and the fact that he just might hang for murder. Unsure of what the laws were in this foreign country, he didn't care for the thought of spending time in a prison either.

"I said what's your name?"

"Smith," the man said. "Max Smith."

Stephen suspected the man was lying, so reached forward and rifled through his pockets, finding a small leather pouch. The contents revealed the name Ryan Evers. "Ryan Evers is more like it, not Max Smith. You'd lie until they stretch your neck tight and your eyes bug out of your head. Come on, get up."

Stephen stood and reached down to pull Evers up. Nearly to his feet, Evers charged forward — a raging bull — driving his head into Stephen's stomach, pushing him back against the tree the bullet had ripped through.

Stephen's knees buckled and he gasped as the sudden impact emptied the air from his lungs. Evers slammed his elbow against the side of Stephen's head and Stephen crashed to the ground. Evers grimaced from pain then raised his leg to stomp on Stephen's head.

Stephen glanced up in time to see the bottom of Evers' foot ready to smash into his face. He jerked his head backward and the boot toe caught him on the mouth, instantly numbing his lips. Evers raised his leg for another attempt and Stephen brought a knee up hard and caught Evers in the buttock, knocking him off balance. Evers stumbled forward and tried to catch himself with his flattened palm of the arm with the shattered collar bone. He crumbled to the ground but came up quickly to see Stephen on his knees picking up his rifle.

Evers ran wildly through the willows toward the river, and by the time Stephen stood and had the rifle in position, the killer had disappeared from sight.

Stephen moved quietly along the trail paralleling the river, listening for sounds in the brush. He passed the place where Jock had been killed and remembered the rifle he'd leaned against Jock's pack. He returned to it to make certain Evers didn't find it. Carrying both rifles and Evers' pistol, Stephen searched for the killer for three hours, finally giving up the chase and returning to his pack.

Stephen's mouth was swollen from the boot toe that grazed his lips, and he had been tasting blood from a cut inside his upper lip since the ordeal. As he'd done with Evers' rifle, he flung the man's knife into the trees, then hid Jock's rifle beneath the dead leaves below the willows.

Before shouldering his pack, he looked up the trail, wondering how much further to the Gitanmaax village, knowing it was only a day's walk to where Morison waited in the shelter for his mates. He guessed Evers would make his way back to Morison's camp and wondered what kind of story he would tell.

Stephen considered walking back downriver to see if Evers did make it, but decided he would be no further threat to the route exploration. He knew Evers lived in San Francisco and the police could track him down later if the man happened to make it back. Swallowing hard, he knew he must push on and complete his task, alone.

CHAPTER 6

MARIANA VEGA RECEIVED STEPHEN'S LETTER THE SAME DAY JOCK was murdered. Her mother, Leena, handed her the envelope and Mariana knew who'd written it before reading Stephen's name on the return address.

Not expecting a letter, she was curious to read the words he may have found in his heart to tell her. She retreated to the living room to be alone, anxiously tearing open the envelope. Mariana didn't notice her mother move near the kitchen door, watching. Then Mariana's expression changed. Finished reading, Mariana turned her face toward the ceiling and lowered the letter to her lap.

Sitting quietly with her thoughts, her eyes misted, and she struggled to hold back the tears, finally lowering her head to stare at the letter. She looked toward the kitchen to see her mother watching. Mariana rose from the couch and walked toward her. Leena reached for Mariana's hands, offering comfort.

"Stephen is confused, mama. I must talk to papa about him." Leena nodded in understanding and released her hands.

Mariana went through the back door and across the hard dirt yard to where Javier lay on the cot reading, as he often did. She sat on the edge of the cot, and when he looked up from the book, she handed him the letter. As he read it, a frown wrinkled his weathered forehead. Finished reading, he gave a questioning sigh.

"What must I do, papa? I thought you may know his feelings for his missing wife. Will he always feel this way?" she asked, then finished in a harsh tone. "She will never come back to him!"

"Mi pequeña niña," he said, placing a hand on her cheek, "I know your heart is hurting from his words, and I know his heart was sad to write them for you to read. He is very fond of you, Mariana. I could see it when he was here, and you can feel it in the way he fumbles at trying to tell you in writing. But you must give him time to deal with memories in his house and in his bed each night. Especially, I think, after spending time with you." He smiled warmly and she leaned down and hugged him.

"Thank you, papa. I will give him time. He has another two and a half months."

Constantly thinking of the morning's frightful incident, Stephen didn't travel far that day. The unrelenting rain and a slippery mud laden trail required great effort to continue the pace. At an early camp, he boiled a piece of dried jerked meat and with a biscuit known as hardtack, he ate slowly and drank from the broth, saving half the liquid for morning. He lay beneath the canvas canopy and thought of the trek ahead, swiping at the occasional larger than usual mosquito which made its way through the rain to share his lean-to shelter, and his blood.

He proceeded with the painstaking task of entering the day's events into the journal, spelling out the reason for Jock's murder. He wanted the telegraph company, the world, to know that the communication race to Europe included murder. Unsure if the company laying the cable across the Atlantic Ocean had hired the man in the buckskin jacket, he wondered who else would benefit from a delay in construction.

After journal entries were made and he was alone on the trail for the first time, he realized how lonely a man must get after months of isolation. His thoughts drifted to Mariana. He envisioned holding her in his arms and smelling her shiny black hair and the fragrance of the bare skin of her neck. He finally fell asleep, still holding her tightly at her front door.

Stephen continued north along the Skeena River, passing through a large Indian village laid out on both banks of the river, a small rock canyon between them. The village known as Kitselas had nearly five hundred people living in the large houses, some not far from the river's edge. The normally wide river narrowed to seventy five-feet and flowed swiftly between the restrictive rock walls. Several large dark coloured basaltic boulders protruded above the water, which rushed wildy around them, creating the noise he'd heard a mile downriver. Several natives from both sides of the canyon watched curiously as he followed the trail along the canyon rim.

The rain stopped before he'd entered the village, and as clouds lifted, he thrilled at seeing the high mountains surrounding the valley. He crossed several small streams flowing out of the mountain's deep canyons before coming to a major junction in the river. The main river flowed from the north, and Stephen felt certain the larger of the two was the Skeena, remembering the map in Conway's office and the roughly drawn one he carried.

The other river, over half the size of the Skeena, flowed from the east, and Conway had called it the Wa Dzun Kwuh.

It was at this junction that the trail had passed through a large treeless flat at the junction and several wood frames that allowed thatching or sewn hides to be spread on top for shelter were set up. Two were made for teepee shelters, as he had seen when crossing the plains to California. From the great numbers of fire-pits, Stephen could tell this was a major meeting place of the Indians.

The large flat sat within the Gitxsan[7] territory and here the Gitxsan traded with other tribes, particularly the Tahltans who came from the north, the Nisga'a and Haida from the coast, and the Wet'suwet'en from further inland to the east. During the trading period, the entire fifty acre flats became a beehive of activity with games of chance, skill, and strength. Dances in full regalia occurred along with singing of the *Adaawk*, the history of their ancestors. There were meetings of the chiefs, feast of natures abundant foods, the exchange of recipies among the women, the playful laughter of children, and the young vraves vying for the attention of maidens.

The area they now travelled was within the Gitxsan tribal territorial boundaries, covering nearly one-tenth of the entire colony. Over three-hundred years earlier, the Gitxsan had been a peaceful nation, until the Ts'imlaxyip people began hunting groundhog in one of the Gitxsan clans' territories. The groundhog was one of the main staples for certain native clans, and the hunting grounds were a sacred possession. This territorial trespass started a nearly three-hundred year-long period of hostilities between several territories, but by 1865, when Frank and Roger arrived, hostilities had subsided to occasional incidents of trespass hunting.

Stephen saw a village on the north side of the rivers' confluence, certain it was Gitanmaax. The main trail he had travelled headed eastward and followed the Wa Dzun Kwuh. The lesser travelled trail continued to the edge of the river where Stephen hoped native canoes were tied, but there were none. Perhaps the trail leading upriver would take him to a crossing.

Following the trail, he climbed to the top of a deep canyon and a mile beyond where the river made a sharp bend north. Gaining a clearer vantage of the canyon ahead, an unexpected sight came into view. An odd shaped bridge a hundred and fifty feet long spanned the deep canyon at one of the narrower reaches. The bridge ends appeared to be set in the rock walls, perhaps fifty feet above the water. An elderly native man stood a short distance onto the bridge, gazing down at the swift flowing water below. Walking further, he spotted several lodges on one of the benches just above the river. The village was called Hagwilget[8]— place of the quiet people—occupied by the Wet'suwet'en[9] Indians, who had received permission to live there from the Gitxsan.

The trail led directly to the top of the canyon above the bridge, then split off. A well-worn trail wound its way down to the bridge, and another headed back downstream to the village nestled at the base of the rock ledge and nest to the river. Stephen leaned his rifle against a tree and struggled to take the heavy wood-frame pack from his aching shoulders. The sudden relief of the load caused him to stagger. Struggling to regain his balance, he knocked a rock over the edge, striking the wood bridge with a loud whack. Startled, the old man looked toward the noise, then up at Stephen. He stared without expression while Stephen stood upright, gave a small wave, and smiled apologetically. The old man saw Stephen's large pack against the tree and shook his head back and forth. Stephen thought the old fellow may be making fun of his clumsiness, but as he intermittently continued shaking his head while looking up, Stephen directed his attention to the pack, wondering what concerned the old man. Finally, the native walked to the end of the bridge and slowly climbed the trail to the top. He looked at Stephen and spoke while pointing at the pack, then to the bridge, shaking his head back and forth while flailing the air with his hand.

When the old man had spoke his piece, Stephen gave a puzzled expression, held his hands outward slightly and shrugged his shoulders unknowingly. The old man's wide grin showed his missing front teeth, which made Stephen like the old fellow right away. He motioned for Stephen to sit, pointed at the bridge and made a sweeping motion toward the other end, then turned to Stephen and waved his finger back and forth while shaking his head. He turned and walked toward the village.

Stephen sat where he could study the construction of the foot bridge. He'd never seen anything like it, wondering how it stayed in place. It had been constructed from two large poles imbedded in the rock wall, protruding out from the cliff thirty feet toward the center of the river. Two other poles stuck out from below the first, angling down slightly, about five feet apart at their ends. Other poles were then lashed to these, joining the four long poles extending from the opposite side with vertical brace poles every five feet or so between the horizontal ones. The lashing appeared to be rope like, made from the inner bark of cedar trees. The width of the bridge appeared to be six feet, and Stephen wondered if they'd ever tried taking a horse over the bridge, seeing the inevitable melee in his mind. He marveled at the ingenuity of these native people, who had none of the advantages of the formal education of the white men, nor of their materials.

Stephen waited twenty minutes, starting to think the old Indian just didn't want him using their bridge. About to retrace his steps back down to the river junction to see if he could yell across the river to the village for help, he saw the old man returning with a younger man. Stephen stood up and waited for them, glancing into the canyon at the murky water still high and dirty from the hard rains.

"Where going?" the younger man said. It surprised Stephen to hear English spoken, but he was happy to hear it.

Stephen answered by speaking slowly, drawing his words out, and using his hands as partial sign language. "I'm going far up Skeena River," he motioned with a squiggly hand. "Find trail for telegraph wire...speak to friend far away," he said, making an attempt to describe it with his hands.

The young man smiled at the hand signals, then answered with a strange accent and strong emphasis on certain words, but plain enough to be understood. "You mean explore for overhead telegraph line coming soon."

Stephen felt embarrassed, the way he had with Mariana, assuming a different coloured skin could not understand plainly spoken English. "Yes, that's just why I'm here. I couldn't cross the river down where the two come together. Is it all right if I cross your wonderful bridge here?"

"Grandfather worried your pack is too heavy to cross with one man carrying it. Thinks you might break through. Some cross pieces are old. Too much weight, one might not hold." He leaned down to test the weight of the pack, but found it too heavy without straddling it and using all his arms strength to get it off the ground. "May be right. Has a sense about these things. I help take it across. Even out the weight."

"Yes, thank you," Stephen said, nodding approval.

The young man said he'd return soon, then walked toward the village.

Stephen wondered if he had knowledge of the terrain and trails further up the Skeena, deciding to ask when he returned. He looked to see the old fellow standing over the pack, looking down, wondering what all it contained.

Mostly grey haired, the man stood under five feet in height. He had a flat broad nose and his face dished in more than Stephen had seen on anyone before, making the cheek bones look large. His skin appeared weathered from long years of being outdoors, and Stephen wondered just how old he was.

The old man nudged at the pack with the toe of his worn leather moccasin, attempting to lift a corner, but it proved too heavy to budge. Stephen thought about what he had near the top of the pack he could give the old man, and remembered the jerky. He untied the cover and folded it back, and the old-timer leaned in closer.

Stephen struggled to break off a piece of the thin dried meat, finally putting it in his mouth, working it back and forth in his clenched teeth. It gave way with a sudden jerk. Stephen smiled and handed the rest toward the old native. The old man looked at the hard dried meat for a moment, then up at Stephen, smiling, showing the large space from his missing front teeth. Then he mimicked Stephen's earlier actions, holding up his hands slightly, and with a widening grin, shrugged his shoulders.

Stephen broke into laughter, placing a hand on the old man's shoulder, which caused the Indian to break out in laughter too. Stephen returned the jerky to the pack, wondering what else he could give his new friend, then remembered Jock's remaining piece of rope, and held it out toward the old-timer.

His eyes widened as he reached out, placed his hands beneath the rope and took it gently as if it would break. He'd seen a rope like this before when fur traders came to the village. He couldn't imagine what kind of tree bark or grass would produce such a fine rope as this. He was thinking of ways to put it to use and when he decided the best one, he looked at Stephen and gratefully showed the missing teeth. Stephen grinned back, nodding his head.

The young man returned with a ten-foot pole and laid it on top of Stephen's pack. "We tie your pack to pole and each take end to cross bridge."

The old man offered use of his new possession. Stephen pulled another piece of rope from the pack, and the two worked together to tie the pack firmly to the pole.

The old Indian asked the younger where Stephen was going, and upon hearing far up the Skeena, he spoke anxiously. Stephen listened carefully, but understood only one word, Bukwas, the same word Jock used to describe the frightening howl they'd heard while loading the sternwheeler with wood. Bukwas were wild people, he'd said, devils that carried off children and ate them.

"What did he say?" Stephen asked.

"No worry. He thinks of old days too much. When he lived up Skeena at Kisgaga'as. He tells village children many old stories. Scares them into being good. We go now," and motioned across the bridge.

"No, wait. I heard him say Bukwas. Tell me what you know about Bukwas. Is it real? Has he ever seen one?"

The young man hesitated. Not all the natives believed the stories his grandfather told and he had seen young men laugh and ridicule the old fellow. They said he ate the red mushroom that makes people see strange things. He did not want the white man to laugh at his grandfather. But yet, this stranger seemed to know the native name. "What you know of Bukwas?"

"I think I heard one on the coast when we gathered wood. It was a strange, scary sound. None of us knew what kind of animal made it."

"No, it no animal! I have seen it. Bukwas no animal."

"What then?" Stephen asked. "Is it a man? I'm told it stands on two legs, leaves big manlike tracks."

"No…it not man like you and me, different…but not animal. I do not want to speak of it. We go now," and the young man picked up the end of the pole with his back toward Stephen.

The bridge had a natural bow in the middle and walking behind the young Indian, Stephen wondered about the weight of the two with the heavy pack between them. The bridge bounced as they walked, and the steps the young men took were short and slow; selecting the strongest cross pieces to step on. Stephen felt relieved to place his feet on solid earth again, and even more so when the two men climbed to the top of the canyon.

Working to untie the rope, he asked the man if he was familiar with trails up the Skeena and on beyond, toward Buck's Bar. The young man didn't recognize the name, Buck's Bar, but had been on several hunting trips up the Skeena with his father and grandfather. He told Stephen the people in Kuldo Village would be most familiar with the trails further up the Skeena and beyond, as it was their hunting territory. Stephen asked if he would need a guide to Kuldo and was told if he followed the trail along the east side of the river, it would lead to the Babine River, and another similar bridge. Kitsagas Village[10] would be just across the river, and from there the trail would lead to Kuldo. He also told Stephen of another trail on the west side of the Skeena, leading from the Kispiox Village to Kuldo. This is the trail Stephen would take, beginning his exploration where the last telegraph line explorer left off upriver from the Kispiox Village.

He handed the rope to the young Indian, asking him to give it back to the grandfather, and thanked the man for his help.

After the young man returned across the foot bridge, Stephen waved farewell and the two natives returned the gesture. Shouldering the pack and picking up his rifle, he started along the trail back downriver toward Gitanmaax Village.

Halfway along the high north rim of the canyon and no trees to obstruct the view, one of the most picturesque mountains imaginable lay across the river to the south. Stephen had previous glimpses of the mountain through the many spruce, birch, poplar and cottonwood trees, but could never see all of it at one time.

Known as *"Stekyooden"* or "Stands Alone" in one native language, and "Mountain of Rolling Rock" in another, trappers who'd gazed upon the mountain, which resembled the great Matterhorn, called it *"Roche Deboule,"* French for tumbling rock.

The coniferous timberline lay two thirds up the steep, nearly vertical slope which ascended over a mile above the valley. Three long narrow serpentine chutes of slide rock ran through the timber from near the top of the mountain to the valley floor; their ten to thirty-foot wide pathways through the tall trees seemed to illustrate how the mountain had obtained its name. A massive chunk of a solid stone cliff had clearly fallen away in pieces over the centuries. Particulary in spring, one could hear the rocks, loosened by the freezing and thawing acts of nature, tumble down the mountain into the chutes. From his vantage point, Stephen could see rugged, craggy peaks on each side of the main mountain, sloping upwards, culminating at a point above and behind it. This majestic mountain was one sight Stephen did not want to forget, so he made a sketch of it in the back of his journal.

Upon his entrance into Gitanmaax Village, the dogs came out in numbers, announcing his presence. One proved aggressive and Stephen kept the rifle barrel pointed toward the dog's feet, holding it at bay. The natives did nothing to quiet the yapping dogs. Strangers were not necessarily welcome, depending on what they brought to the village to trade. Four years earlier, one had brought smallpox, devastating the population.

He continued through the village, searching for the trading post Conway had told him about, a quarter of a mile upstream. Surrounded by a few settlers cabins, the community was named Hazelton within a few months of Stephen's arrival.

Stephen noticed a small shed with smoke billowing out beneath its roof. He stopped, thinking the shed was on fire and looked around for someone to shout at and let them know, but saw no one. Then he noticed a second shed of similar size smoking profusely, but no one seemed concerned about that fire either. Seeing a rack of salmon filets near the shed, he realized the sheds were smoke houses, full of fresh caught salmon from the Skeena River.

He located the log building with the Hudson's Bay sign on front and removed his pack, placing it at the edge of the doorway so he could see it from inside, as he'd been advised. He entered a small dark store with limited stock on the rough board shelves.

The large man behind the counter looked up, watching Stephen take in the supplies. He had a thick brown full beard and moustache with tobacco juice stains evident in both. Stephen suspected they were not from one day of chewing, and a wad made the trader's cheek bulge. He closed the book he'd been reading.

"Well you look about out of place as a man can be, stranger," the burly man said with a raspy voice. "You must be one of them fellers' here because of that tele...whatever line that's coming."

"Yes sir, and it's called a telegraph line. That's the reason I'm here. I'm headed up north, so I stopped to pick up a couple of supplies. Do you have any jerked meat or pemmican on hand?."

"Dried meat? Hell, no. Haven't had any all summer. The shipment that came upriver a few months ago didn't bring half my order. That's why my shelves are so bare. Damn company expects me to make a profit. Can't do it if they don't give me what I ask for. What else you needing?"

"Do you have any bacon and flour?"

"Bacon? Hell, no! Nobody wants to raise pigs up here. It's a $1.20 a pound when I did have it a while back, but nobody could afford it." He spat into a container behind the counter. "Flour I got. How much you needing?"

"I only need a pound," Stephen replied, disappointed in the lack of dried meat. "Is there any kind of meat I can buy until I get upriver a ways? Haven't seen much game so far."

The storekeeper moved to the flour barrel and weighed out the flour. "Ever had smoked salmon?" he asked.

"No, I haven't. I've had fresh steelhead trout from a river in California. Taste anything like that?"

"Ohhh, lots better if it's smoked right. Keeps a long time too. You'll have to go to Mishka's. She has the best fish and should have some smoked up. They were netting good catches before the rain brought the river up. What you got to trade her?"

"I've got money," Stephen said. "Will she take money?"

"Don't do her much good if there's nothing to buy, friend. Didn't you bring something to trade with the Indians? Is this your first time in the north woods or something?"

"Well, yes, I did bring a few trade items. I'd hoped to save them for the Indians further north. I've got a little coloured cloth and some knives. All made in San Francisco."

"She'll trade for either. Here's your flour, that's sixty cents. Anything else?"

Stephen asked for cartridges for the .32 caliber pistol taken from Evers. Able to buy ten, he slipped them into a pant pocket. Receiving directions to Mishka's house, he shouldered the pack and walked the wide dusty trail with rifle in one hand and bag of flour in the other, thinking he would stow the flour and cartridges when he dug the knives and cloths from his pack.

He hadn't considered that Mishka spoke no English, and after much sign language—fish swimming upriver, eating fish, rubbing the stomach then pulling out the knives and coloured cloth—Mishka understood. Tasting a sample of the smoked salmon, he smiled, nodded, and held up two fingers. She in turn took all his coloured cloth and two of his best knives.

Stephen made camp two miles up the Skeena, far enough to be out of range of barking dogs. For supper he ate warmed smoked salmon, boiled rice, and a couple of drop biscuits cooked in a covered frying pan. Although burnt on the bottom and slightly gooey in the middle, he convinced himself they were quite good.

Sleeping with his head beneath the blanket to escape the numerous mosquitos, he awoke to a sun well above the high mountains surrounding the valley. Squinting and wiping the sleep from one eye that wouldn't open, then rubbing again, he realized it was swollen nearly shut. Scratching a itch on his lower arm revealed a puffy area there, too. Wondering what caused the swelling, he looked closely at his arm, seeing a tiny red spot at the center of the swollen area—his introduction to the blood thirsty mosquitoes' competition for the vein—the annoying black fly. He would experience many more bites over the next few weeks.

After a breakfast of slapjacks, Stephen struck camp and before noon came to the junction of the Kispiox River on the opposite side of the Skeena. The trail continued upriver a quarter mile where Stephen found two canoes on the shore. Across the river set the sizable village of Kispiox, "the hiding place."

The canoes were not as large as those in which he'd started up the Skeena. These were only ten-feet long, hollowed out of a cottonwood tree. Hoping he wouldn't leave someone stranded by taking a canoe to the other side, he loaded his pack and pushed out into the wide river.

Never having paddled a canoe before and sitting too far toward the back, he swirled in circles, as he experimented with the paddle. Laughing at himself, he moved forward until he found the proper weight distribution, then paddled frantically as he moved swiftly downriver. He heard laughter from the opposite bank and saw three teenage Indian girls watching and pointing at him as he passed by. He felt embarrassed they had witnessed his clumsy launch.

Dipping the paddle deep and pulling hard, he floated out of the faster Skeena water just as he reached the mouth of the Kispiox River. Having seen two canoes near where the girls were standing, he pulled the canoe back upstream and onto the bank by the others. The girls walked toward the village as he neared, looking back as they followed the trail through the low brush and high grass.

Stephen wondered if he should go into the village or skirt around the east side and find the trail north on his own. Deciding it would be best for the telegraph company to make his presence and assignment known, he followed the girls toward the village.

At the edge of the village stood an immense building made of large cedar logs. Being much larger than any of the houses in Gitanmaax, he assumed it was a meeting house.

On each side of the longhouse doorway stood a sixty-foot cedar pole planted firmly in the ground, each differently carved. One had a bird on top and a huge bird head in the middle with human legs and arms. Below were two upside down faces, followed by a large lizard climbing down the pole. The pole on the other side of the door had huge human-like faces with large lips and eyes and flat noses. Each of the five faces had small arms and legs with knees bent inwards, resting on the head below. Beneath the lowest head were figures of children, shoulder to shoulder around the pole. He studied the figures, wondering about their meaning.

These were called totem poles, one depicted a story or myth, the other a memorial to deceased clan chiefs. The birds shown on the one totem pole represented the clan of the eagle, or Lax Xskiik in Gitxsan. The other three clans within the village were Wolf or Lax Gibuu, Frog or Lax Ganeda, and Fireweed or Giskaast. Members of the clan were considered to be related to each other by blood since they were descendants of the same ancestor. A man did not marry a woman from his own clan. Because of intermarriages with other clans, there were individuals within each village who were members of other clans, with the Chief's clan being the predominant crest.

As he stood looking up at each pole, viewing one then the other, inspecting them closely, he didn't notice the middle-aged man standing to the side of the longhouse, watching. Stephen started to walk away and was startled by the man's voice.

"Hey...white man. Where going?" he said, with the same strange accent as the young Indian at the Hagwilget bridge. Stephen turned to face the man, whose facial features were somewhat similar to the Hagwilget men, but did not dish in as much. He wore loose fitting-pants with the legs bunched up over handmade boots and a faded red shirt. A dark blue short-bill wool cap was tipped back above the hairline. Stephen could see a slight resemblance to the Chinese in San Francisco, but with darker skin and less slanted eyes. He wondered where these people had originally come from.

"Hello. I'm glad to run into someone who speaks English here at your village," Stephen said, walking toward the man. "I need to find the trail north and to find where the other telegraph line surveyor ended his survey a few months ago. Can you help me?"

The man hesitated, expressionless, then said, "Why I help you?"

Stephen thought about the question, unable to think of an immediate response. He had no idea of what impression the other surveyor may have left upon the village, good or bad. He decided to answer a question with a question.

"Did another surveyor stop in your village and talk to you or your chief about the telegraph line?" The man didn't reply, just stood there with the same stoic expression. Stephen wondered if all his English words were too many to comprehend. "Did you understand what I said?" he asked.

"Understand words, white man. Not know why I help."

Stephen felt frustrated at the response, but made an effort not to show it. He spoke slowly and firmly. "I am new to your area and do not know your language, your customs, your concerns for the land. I was hired to explore a route for the telegraph line, from above your village north along the Skeena and Nass Rivers. It will take me more than two months to explore the route. I am willing to pay for someone like yourself to help. Does that interest you?"

"What you pay?"

"That depends on how well you know the country for three hundred miles to Buck's Bar. Do you know it?"

"Might. How much you pay?"

Stephen became increasingly uncomfortable with the man's responses, thinking he may not make a good guide or travelling companion and made a decision to not use the man. "Like I said, it depends on what you know and I can't seem to get a straight answer. I'll find someone I can talk with in your village."

Stephen walked away, expecting the man to say something more, but there was no response. As he walked through the village in the warm still air, a putrid stench grew strong. A dead dog lay a short distance from one of the houses and a mound of decaying plant matter outside the door of another. The natives seemed indifferent to the smells.

He asked several people where he could find the chief, but they just looked at him without responding, and he realized none of them spoke English. He'd noticed a sadness in the faces of many and heard weeping in two of the houses.

Each house belonged to a village elder, or a person of prominence, and was called "the house of" followed by their name. The large village contained forty to fifty houses and in each house lived ten to twenty people, immediate family members, aunts, uncles and cousins. Stephen guessed about seven or eight hundred people lived in the village. He thought it a strange society, different than any he'd seen before.

As he moved through the village he noticed the three teenage girls standing in a doorway, pointing, giggling, and whispering to one another.

"Where is chief?" he hollered in their direction, but they only giggled at the strange words. He smiled back at them, especially the one with the engaging face and long black hair. She reminded him of Mariana.

This village also had smoke houses leaking grey puffs of smoke just below their roofs, as well as its share of dogs, several still yapping behind as he came to the end of the village, beyond which lay dense forest with thick undergrowth. He needed to find the trail leading north, which would take him to the end of the previous survey, as shown on the map and surveyor notes Conway had given him.

He went east toward the Skeena River, looking for the trail. Just as he spotted it, two men, each carrying a large salmon on a stick over their shoulder, stepped into the clearing along the trail. They'd come from a short distance up the Kispiox River where rock ledges lined the inside of a sharp horseshoe bend. Their wooden fish weir produced the fresh fish for smoking or cooking over an open fire for the evening's meal.

The men stopped, staring at Stephen as he waited to enter the trail. The younger man in the lead turned to the other and spoke. The older man responded with a laugh, and they continued walking toward the village. Stephen watched them walk away, wondering what they had said about him. He heard them laugh again a short distance away.

Stephen lowered his heavy pack to the ground, rubbing the tops of his shoulders to relieve aching muscles. He retrieved the map showing the end point of the previous survey and studied it while he sat at the edge of the village clearing. He took a deep drink of the fresh water from his canvas water bag, filled at last night's camp. Before taking a second drink, he thought of the possibility of not finding a stream of clear water before making camp for the night, so pushed the cork back in the hole.

"How much you pay?" the voice said from behind. Stephen jumped at the sound of the voice, turning his head quickly. The man wearing the dark blue cap had followed and crept up on Stephen without his hearing.

"I found the trail," Stephen replied. "My map will show me how to get to Kuldo Village. I will hire someone there."

"You travel through Bukwas ground. None in Kuldo take you there. They afraid. I not afraid. How much you pay?"

There was that reference again to the wild devil giant, Stephen thought. Seemed like he just couldn't get away from it. He knew it wasn't true, but there *was* that strange howling noise on the coast. Oh well, he thought, some legends just seem to hang around. He wanted to change the subject and remembered the sadness of the people in the village, so asked about it.

"A village woman and daughter, pick the red berries from the ground bush," the native replied. "Grizzly chase them. Daughter run faster. Bear catch woman. Kill her. Young men of village find that bear. Kill him and cut him in pieces for other bears to see. Carve hunter's face in four trees around bear parts, so other bears know who kill that bear and cut him up. Those bears like white man to eat too. You pay me good, I don't let them eat you. I don't let Bukwas eat you, too. How much you pay?"

"No thanks," Stephen said, "I won't need to be protected from the bear or your legends. If I see the Bukwas though, I will tell him you wanted to come with me, that you are not afraid of him," and gave a pacifying grin, nodding his head slightly.

Visibly irritated by Stephen's response, the man started for the village, his pants riding low on his hips, baggy in the back, the front cinched below his large belly. Stephen wondered how they kept from falling down as the man walked and he had a vision of a large duck waddling away.

The following day, Stephen came to a sharp bend in the Kispiox River where a small stream entered from the north through a clearing. A tall single spruce tree stood in the opening as shown on the map, marking the end of the previous exploration. He found a large "T" blaze in the spruce the other surveyor had marked by cutting through the bark. This would be Stephen's starting point, and he felt relieved that he could finally start what he'd been hired to accomplish.

CHAPTER 7

WHILE UNPACKING HIS SURVEY EQUIPMENT AT CAMP THAT EVENING, Stephen felt encouraged. After dark he took observations of the North Star to determine the azimuth. The following morning he took readings on the sun to obtain the latitude and approximate longitude using a sextant, an instrument normally found on ships at sea. This allowed his starting point to be a physical, fixed position, both on the ground and on the map he would be making while going along the exploration route.

Each subsequent sextant reading would give him a new physical position from which he could update the map and verify compass directions to estimated positions of major features: mountain peaks, prominent hills, ridge lines, stream crossings and directions of water flow. Hugh had supplied the sextant and instructed Stephen on its use, informing him that explorers Lewis and Clark had used a similar instrument on their epic journey across the continent.

Stephen's starting point from the initial readings were determined from mathematical calculations; the results being somewhat different from those of the previous explorer, as shown in the surveyors notes from Conway. Stephen double checked his recorded readings and calculations, finding them correct.

Anxious to begin, Stephen commenced the exploration at 5:00 a.m. He checked the compass often to see if the Indian trail kept a course he believed paralleled the Skeena River, uncertain of the true course of the river due to the numerous trees.

The ground he traversed proved relatively flat with occasional small ravines running toward the Kispiox River, which flowed near the west side of the valley. The underbrush grew thick with alders, preventing him from seeing more than fifty feet in any direction. A couple of times each day, he made side trips to higher hills, hoping for a view of the surrounding terrain. He took notes and made sketches from each vantage point, recorded tree species and average sizes, noting if there were adequate numbers for telegraph poles. At the beginning, there were only tree-covered hills to the west, but these eventually turned into mountain peaks as the valley narrowed. To the east across the Skeena lay an immense mountain range with high craggy peaks. At the end of the day, he estimated he had travelled only seven miles in the dense undergrowth.

Stephen saw few bear droppings in the underbrush, who seemingly waited to leave their droppings on trails, as if they were personally cleared pathways for that purpose. He also noticed a difference in the size between the black bear's dung and the larger dung piles he assumed to be from grizzlies, some as large as horse droppings. Never having seen a grizzly, he estimated the size to be at least twice that of black bears in Virginia and back in California.

He saw frequent coyote droppings on the trail, mostly full of hair, and also saw numerous round cylinder shaped droppings in the alder brush he thought to be from wapiti, which he'd seen in north central California. But then he spotted a cow moose and calf in the timber and finding where they'd bedded, he nudged the droppings with his toe, knowing he was mistaken about elk. This was his first sighting of moose and he marveled at their long gangly legs and their swift movement through the trees.

While travelling up the lower Skeena several days before, the bear droppings showed evidence of fish bones and skin as well as berry seeds, but further north they were mostly berries. He deduced that bears would soon be coming down from the mountains to fish the rivers full of spawning salmon.

It was the second week of August, and the large chinook salmon had been in the river for over a month. The smaller silvers, sockeyes and humpback salmon were just coming in with the high water. The numerous humpbacks spawned in shallower water and were a major food source for bears, being easier to grab with their strong teeth, thus supplying them with fattening nutrition in preparation for winter hibernation.

The hot August days brought out black flies by the thousands. Less noticeable when walking, the hordes surrounded Stephen's head whenever he stopped, causing him to brush them off his hands and face constantly. They were unrelenting, like raindrops when you didn't want to get wet and had no shelter to get under. The fast, darting flies were most irriting when they flew into his ears and occasionally one would get sucked in his mouth when he was breathing hard, causing him to retch to keep from swallowing it. They found their way into his clothing at the shirt cuffs and collar, and up his pant legs. Usually he didn't even know they'd taken their fill of blood until later on when the bites began to itch. The small bites usually left a pin-head size, dark red mark surrounded by a lighter red area half the size of Stephen's fingernail, unless they puffed up as his eye had done. They began to itch the following day, and he scratched at them often, the irritation of each bite lasting up to four days.

The only thing he found to stave off the flies attacks was to rub mud on his exposed skin and dampened tea leaves in his cuffs and collar. His mud splattered face gave the appearance of an Indian warrior prepared for battle. In the evenings after washing off the mud and preparing supper, he examined the bites, numerous enough to look like measles. Then, mosquitoes took their turn at feasting on his blood, and he grew a strong hatred for biting insects.

Often when he walked off the trail seeking better vantage points to take compass bearings to prominent mountain peaks, he waded through numerous patches of wild rose bushes. The thorns easily penetrated his pants, embedding in his skin. At camp, he dug them out with the needle from his small sewing kit, some thorns being a quarter of an inch long. The reddened areas from thorn pricks added to the appearance of measles.

One late afternoon, Stephen came to a large burn, an area overrun by fire several years ago. This was the largest open area he'd seen since leaving the coast, other than the lush green meadows above the 5,000 foot timberline. He estimated the burn to be five miles across and noted this in his journal, as poles would need to be hauled to the area for the telegraph line.

Berries were ripe and numerous in the burn, and he spent more than an hour gathering and eating the small sweet strawberries growing in clusters on ground plants and raspberries on their prickly stems. He filled a small cooking pot with berries and placed it in the pack, wrapped in a shirt.

Nearly across the burn, he topped a small knoll, startling a light brown bear cub with a slight hump on its front shoulders. The cub whirled and ran downhill, bawling as if it were injured. Seventy yards below, the cub's mother stood on her hind legs and Stephen heard the 'woof' from the huge grizzly sow.

She dropped to all fours and ran swiftly uphill to protect her cub. Stephen could only see the back of the large bear above the waist high vegetation as its muscled body rippled with each placement of her front feet.

Stephen dropped the pack as quickly as he could, trying not to take his eyes off the bear. He couldn't believe how fast it ran up the hill, and in a matter of seconds it was nearly on top of him, stopping no less than five feet away. The sow immediately stood on her hind legs, and although downhill from him, her eyes looked down into his. The rifle did not yet have a cartridge in the chamber, the charge happening so swiftly. As he prepared to close the breach, she reached her snout toward him, giving a tremendous roar, plainly showing her four long teeth only three feet from Stephen's face.

Fear shot through his entire being. The strong odor from the bear's breath enveloped his nostrils, and he thought it may be the last thing he would ever smell again. The roar was deafening, seeming to last an eternity. He visioned the attack Javier Vega had described, the bear going after his head first to immobilize him.

Stephen thought of Mariana and knew he would not see her again. She would never know what happened to him. He knew too, he would never know what happened to Rachel and Michael, and he'd never be able to tell Hugh of his exploration experience. He felt sorrow that he'd seen his niece and nephew one time only. All these thoughts happening in seconds, even though it seemed time had stood still.

The sow appeared as though her chest muscles were tightened, and her beady eyes glared in anger. Then the threatening roar subsided, and she pulled her head back slowly. Stephen mustered courage to close the breech on the rifle held at his chest, and the sow looked down at the noise. As if sensing the power held in his hands, she dropped to the ground and made one more threatening gesture, huffing once while swiping the ground with her paw, then turned and slowly walked back down to her waiting cub, leading it toward the Skeena River.

Stephen stood motionless until he could no longer see the bear. She could have laid open the entire side of his face with one swipe and crushed his skull in her powerful jaws. But she had spared his life, and he could do nothing more than to spare her life too, as she strolled off. He sat on a nearby log for half an hour before the adrenaline completely subsided, and his nerves calmed.

Stephen couldn't believe all the thoughts he had in those short seconds. His first thoughts were of Mariana, and she would be on his mind well into the night. Also he'd thought about Rachel and Michael, and he still missed them a great deal. A large piece of his life had been ripped away. He'd wondered many times what happened to them, if they were still alive or not. And now he thought about the cold, lonely house he'd been coming home to before leaving on this exploration, and what it would be like again when he returned. Then his thoughts drifted back to Mariana and he recalled her scent, her long black hair, and the eagerness of her warm kiss. Swatting mosquitoes by the fire that night he wrote Mariana a second letter, hoping to mail it from Buck's Bar.

Mid-morning found him on a trail leading into a steep canyon where he heard rushing water over rapids. Pushing his way through the heavy undergrowth growing over the trail near the river bank, his leg brushed against one of the broad-leafed plants that stood up to six feet tall. The sharp pain from the swipe against his leg caused him to pull away and shout out. Looking closely at the stem of the plant, he saw many needle-like protrusions. He continued forward slowly, careful to place a foot against the stem of each plant leaning into the trail, forcing it to the ground or pushing it aside until he passed. One plant slipped off his foot and slapped the side of a hand, his hat brim preventing it from striking his face. This prompted a strong cursing of this new type of plant, and he wondered what they called it up here. He spent a moment attempting to pick the tiny barbed slivers from his flesh, but most of the tips remained beneath the skin's surface. The leg continued to sting and he dropped his pants to examine the red spot, rubbing the pants together at the impact point to break apart any slivers in the material. He hoped the stinging would subside soon.

He cautiously worked through the patch and onto the river bank. The trail led upstream over considerable downfall, and he saw only swift deep water in the Kuldo River. Downstream travel appeared more promising, so he detoured a quarter mile before finding a shallow crossing.

From the five-foot river bank he could see large salmon in the water below the crossing point. Occasionally one would splash the surface, swim quickly upstream, then turn back downstream, fighting for spawning beds. Further downriver, he could see a large opening through the trees lining both banks. He believed he was seeing the mouth of the Kuldo River where it entered the Skeena. He noticed a steep embankment gouged out of the hillside on the opposite side of the larger river, likely caused by glacial activity from past eons.

He'd spotted several tremendous sized glaciers in the high mountain peaks east of the Skeena, marveling at them each time a clear view presented itself. One of the higher mountains he saw northeast of the Kispiox Village, and he could see still when he looked back to the southeast just before dropping into the steep canyon, was marked 'Thomlinson' on Conway's rough map. Travelling past the peak, he had a panoramic view of a huge glacier, two miles long and a mile wide. From that peak, he suspected one could see at least half the route his exploration would take. The view from up there must be breathtaking with the peak towering a mile and a half above the valley floor. If he only had the time, he could take a few days and climb the mountain.

Crossing the greenish coloured river, a salmon swam swiftly past, nearly brushing Stephen's leg. It appeared to weigh over fifty pounds. The tip of the tail and dorsal fin were turning white from the decaying process that takes place after spawning. The rest of its body would continue to decay and the fish would eventually swim into the calmer water until, actions slowing and strength diminishing, it floated helplessly on its side, and wash against the shore or sank to the bottom, where the fish accumulated in the deep pools.

Eagles, hawks, ravens, gulls and jays picked at the rotting salmon flesh lying amongst the rocks or on sandy beaches. Coyotes, fox, skunks and martin occasionally fed on dead fish, as did bears, which often took only the top of the head. However, bears preferred catching the fresher fish as they spawned in the shallows. He saw many tracks of black and grizzly bears' on the sandy beaches at the water's edge. By late September, the stench near the river would be overpowering with hundreds of decaying fish strewn along the beaches. If heavy rains came, the smell would be washed away in the torrent, the water purifying itself as it flowed over numerous boulders, tumbling its way toward the ocean.

After wading the river, Stephen walked a short way upstream to scout for a good telegraph line crossing, then downriver to the Skeena. He made camp on a sandy beach where several fresh wolf tracks were displayed.

Two of the animals appeared to be huge, their footprints larger than Stephen's fist. What if the pack returned and were hungry? Could he shoot and reload fast enough? He rigged his lean-to shelter with its back toward the river, keeping his rifle nearby.

He craved fresh salmon for supper, so taking the pistol from his pack, he walked back to the river crossing and worked his way slowly into the stream. Picking out a smaller salmon not yet turning a reddish colour, he aimed the pistol and waited for the right moment. The male moved in behind a spawning female in the two-foot deep water, waiting until she turned on her side and flapped her tail violently, fanning out a depression before releasing the eggs in the shallow hollow. The male swam over the eggs and released his milky white sperm. As it neared the surface, its duty complete, Stephen fired the pistol. The fish shuddered and went still, floating on its side just below the surface.

Stephen rushed downstream, attempting to grab the slimy tail with his free hand. Each step splashed water on his clothes and up to his face and the slippery rock covered bottom caused him to fight for balance. The fish kept slipping from his grip, and he would lunge forward again, getting even wetter while thrashing his way downstream. He was intent on seizing the prize.

Finally, he managed to steer it close to shore where he scooped it partway onto the bank. The slimy fish started sliding back into the river, so he kicked at it, causing him to slip on a wet rock. With arms flailing wildly, he tried regaining his balance as the unrehearsed, half-pirouette move sent him splashing into the river. Even in wet clothing, the cold water took his breath. He jumped up quickly, as the salmon floated next to the bank and he splashed after it again, but in slow motion in his soaked and heavy clothing, with the dripping wet pistol in hand. Had some unknown person bear witness to the comical attempts to capture the sizeable fish, Stephen would have certainly heard their laughter.

Capturing his prize and returning to camp, he gathered additional firewood to dry the wet clothes. After delicious salmon steaks and boiled rice, he lay on his bedroll and caught up on his journal and map. Before turning in, he took a pinch of the baking soda he carried in a small tin and scrubbed his teeth with his finger, then swirled it around with a bit of water. This had been a habit since he'd married Rachel, but now he only washed his teeth every four or five days, trying to make the supply last the duration.

Back on the trail, he worked his way along a steep side-hill and through a patch of those broad leaf, needle stem plants and came to a branch in the well-worn trail, one leading toward the Skeena. Thinking he should be nearing the village of Kuldo, he followed the trail to the foot of the hill where a spring creek ran through a small meadow. Several minutes later he could hear children playing, as lodges came into view through the trees.

When he entered the village, the children stopped their play and ran to their homes, pointing and shouting. Adults came to their lodge doors to see what stirred the dogs and excited the children. Stephen nodded, saying hello as he passed each lodge, but no one spoke until he was nearly through the village when a man stepped from the side of a lodge. Stephen stopped, turning toward him.

He was a tall, middle aged man with long dark hair, parted in the middle, the sides covering his ears and shoulders. He wore a grey flannel shirt, brown cotton pants tucked inside rubber boots, with a grey woolen sock over the top of each pant leg.

At the front of his lodge several small animal hides were stretched on frames, and many stretching frames of various sizes hung alongside the building. Behind the lodge, Stephen could see salmon fillets drying in the afternoon sun.

"Can I help you?" the man said in plain English.

Stephen felt relieved to finally find someone with whom to talk. A small boy peeked around the corner of the lodge, and when Stephen looked toward him, he quickly disappeared. Stephen directed his attention back to the man. "Ah...yes. I'm on my way to Buck's Bar on the Stikine River. I was hoping someone here could give me information on the best trails."

"Why are you going up there? All the gold has been mined out."

"Well, actually I'm not looking for gold. I'm doing a survey for a telegraph company. They hope to build a line all the way from the United States, clear past Buck's Bar, and across the Straits to Russia."

"What the heck is a telegraph?" the man asked. "Why don't you take your pack off and tell me what you white men have come up with now?"

Stephen liked the man right off, and as they sat on wood stools outside the lodge, he explained the purpose of the telegraph, gave a rough idea of how it worked and what materials were used in the construction process. The man continued to ask questions, nodding in understanding after Stephen's explanation. He invited Stephen to stay the night, and they talked late.

He went by the name Kwabellem and had lived in the Kuldo Village all his life. Not only did he have knowledge of the trails to Buck's Bar but was well versed on the white man's customs and many inventions.

He'd become acquainted with white trappers in the early 1840s. His interest in trapping had drawn him to learn their language, and he spent as much time with them as they allowed. In early spring when the ice had gone out, he began selling his own furs to traders who'd travelled up the Skeena as far as Kispiox Village.

Kwabellem had travelled to the coast on several occasions where he traded beaver pelts and moose and caribou hides for trapping supplies and guns for the village. Each trip, the party of travelers brought back eulachon oil used for lamps extracted from a small tasty ocean fish and eaten with various foods. In springtime, at a place called Fishery Bay at tidewater's end on the Nass River, miles of huts were strung along the shore lines. Three nations—Haida, Tlinkit, and Tsimsyan—gathered for the candle fish harvesting and for barter. The native women would squeeze oil from the small fish by pressing them between their bare breasts, tradition not allowing use of their hands. A trade route known as the Grease Trail extended into the interior, and large amounts of the candle fish oil was traded.

Some of the traps Kwabellem had traded for were used for groundhogs, or marmots, which the Kuldo people relished as part of their diet. The marmots were found at the north end of their hunting territory on the plateaus where rock outcrops were scattered about, giving the furry animals ample dens and hiding places. These were the small hides Stephen had seen stretched out on the side of Kwabellem's lodge.

Kwabellem also told Stephen of the small lake on the east side of the Skeena called Dumsumlow, or Lake of Monsters. He warned Stephen to never go there, it being a place of death many years ago. Headless people now wandered the forest around the lake, and it was not unusual to see a large sailing ship floating silently when moonbeams reflected off the water.

Stephen stayed in the village another day and Kwabellem introduced him to many of the villagers. Stephen also gained the friendship of

Kwabellem's grandson, the little boy who'd peeked around the corner, and only a year older than Michael would be. The child had been named Laelt, or "snake," by his father who had died from smallpox four years ago. Kwabellem's daughter came back to Kuldo from Gitanmaax, and Kwabellem started calling the youngster Kuhnelawp, or "always casting stones," because of the boy's inexhaustible habit of picking up rocks and chucking them at trees or flowers. Kuhnelawp followed the two men around the village, asking questions whenever he wasn't sidetracked by winging a small stone that couldn't be passed up.

Kwabellem noticed the swollen red mark on Stephen's hand, telling him it was from the Devil's Walking Stick, and that it would probably fester and fill with pus, needing to be squeezed to get the small poisonous barbs out. Stephen remarked that it was a good name for the treacherous plant.

Kwabellem talked about his people and of their ability to withstand suffering circumstances. They seemed to bear extremes of cold, heat, hunger, and exposure with greater fortitude than white men. He mentioned, too, that although there were thieves amongst his people, for they did not deem it dishonorable to steal, they only stole from others outside their totem, but seldom from a stranger.

Stephen noticed the people had considerable respect for age. An older woman had attained great influence in the clan as a seer, or fortune teller, and several women held the position of village elder, sitting with respect in the longhouse when council fires burned. The natives were fond of and indulgent to their children, rarely chastising them. The women seemed modest or reserved and had a decorous bearing. The men were humble and relaxed. They laughed amongst themselves often. Most of the villagers had large dark eyes, flat foreheads, large cheek bones and small, flat, broad noses. Here too, they seemed indifferent to the stench of decaying animals and rancid grease. Only one man appeared to harbor hostility toward white men, the results of an unpleasant encounter with miners passing through to the goldfields at Buck's Bar.

Stephen asked Kwabellem to be his guide, but Kwabellem was to join a caribou hunting party in the higher mountains, where there were many rolling grassy ridges. However, he did draw a map of the trails and landmarks Stephen would encounter, confident that he should be able to find Buck's Bar.

Kwabellem told Stephen he'd been invited by Chief Clahquilhut to be his guest for dinner, a way of expressing pleasure at the white man's presence.

The chief's lodge was a large square structure sided with thick cedar planks, split with wooden wedges, ten feet high at the eaves and twenty at the center. A huge fire at the center of the cedar plank floor sat in a recessed square on hard packed earth, the smoke rising through a large open vent, which could be opened or closed, at the roof's peak. Around the walls hung several old rifles, a few traps, animal skins and other property indigenous to the native people.

Stephen sat with Kwabellem, next to the chief, while villagers squatted on the floor around the structure, nearly filling it. A young man placed a small wooden trough of clean water in front of Stephen, who followed the chief's example and washed his hands.

The feast began with roasted and boiled salmon and potatoes they'd grown themselves. Next came bear meat, caribou, and beaver, each served with a generous helping of eulachon grease. The feast ended with sopeoolaly, a dried berry stirred vigorously with water, forming a brown foam, relished by the village people, but bitter to Stephen. Not wanting to offend his host, he smiled with each small bite, trying not to squint from the unpleasant taste.

The chief declared a dance in honor of their guest. The dancers queued behind a master of ceremonies dressed in a colourful robe painted with small birds and animals and lined with shiny silver pieces of sea shells. Two men began drum beats on sixteen inch round wood frames, covered with a nearly transparent skin on one side. Then a third drum, like a wooden box, having a much deeper tone joined in, keeping an intermittent beat with the others. Three men dressed in animal skins and wooden masks—a bear, an eagle, and a human-like face—danced with slow short steps, then began a chant in unison with the drums. Their postures were a slight squat with rigid joints, the bear man's back bent over. First the large drum then the small drums, and the men shouted "YAAAWHEY" forcefully. BOOM boom, BOOM boom, "YOOOHO", every fourth time. The dance lasted several minutes, each man's costume, prance, and stares into the crowd portrayed something unique and meaningful. Kwabellem leaned over and whispered some of the meanings, but it was difficult for Stephen to hear.

The dance complete, a tribute to past chief's was made by announcement of names and a small amount of fragrant weed placed on the fire.

A second dance, comical in nature, caused much laughter from the audience. The wooden masks of these dancers costumes were two ravens with a long bird beak and a mountain goat with a lengthy pointed goat's nose.

The finalé consisted of up to twenty dancers. Three women in ornate white leather dresses began the dance, joined by children holding feathers. Then finally young men and women, all prancing slowly around the floor, chanting in unison to the same drum beat as the first dance. It was intriguingly beautiful to see, but ended suddenly; every motion ceased, every sound stilled, the master of ceremonies announcing the end of the performance. Everyone quietly left the chief's lodge. Stephen would never forget the magical evening.

He departed the village with a fresh supply of smoked salmon, jerked caribou meat, cooked ground squirrel and a small amount of beaver, leaving behind the remainder of the fresh salmon he'd shot. He also left the remaining knives he'd brought for trading. His spirits high with a map of the trail leading to Buck's Bar, he had a month and a half to complete the survey, return to Kispiox Village and meet the construction crew.

Two days later, Stephen came to a deep gorge with a small, crystal clear stream running swiftly over the boulders. Stopping to fill his water bag and drink the cold water, he noticed a squared piece of wood poking above water, wedged between the rock wall and roots of a dead hemlock tree. He crossed the shallow stream and worked his way over the slippery water spattered boulders to the chunk of wood.

Pulling on it several times before freeing the attached pieces from its wedged hold, he recognized it as the remains of a sluice box used to extract gold from gravel beds. It didn't appear to be old, but might have been preserved by the water. He wondered why the prospector had left it. Perhaps he'd found a lot of gold in the creek and no longer needed it.

He tossed it aside and worked his way up the steep hillside, rather than walking back over the slippery rocks to the trail. He stopped several times before reaching the top, resting his aching legs and catching his breath. At the top, he worked his way through the trees back toward the trail and noticed a light-coloured object seven feet above ground, wedged in the fork of a hemlock tree. It appeared to be the top of a skull, but he could see only a small portion, so he stepped around the tree, flinching at the hideous sight. As he stepped back, he caught a heel on a dead branch and fell backwards on his pack. The pack proved too heavy to stand upright from this position, and he struggled to work his arms out of the shoulder straps, then stood and stared in disbelief.

A partial human skeleton hung down from the fork in the tree. All that remained attached to the skull were the neck bones, part of the spine and a few ribs. The skull was face down in the tree crotch, and the rest of the decayed body had fallen to the ground at the foot of the tree. The clothing had kept the cream-coloured bones from scattering. Pieces of dried flesh clung to areas around the few joints he could see. A pant leg had slipped above the leather jackboots, revealing a leg bone still attached to a foot inside the boot. A pocket watch lay on the ground at the base of the tree.

Stephen couldn't imagine how the poor man's body got into the tree, its skull wedged tightly between the two trunks that ran together no more than three feet below the skull. The man's feet would have been at least two feet above the ground when he hung there. It was impossible to visualize how this could have happened.

He couldn't just leave the skull and neck bones hang like this for someone else to stumble upon, so he searched the area and found a strong dead branch. He raised it up to the neck, pushing upwards, hoping to free the skull. The neck bones gave way and clattered as the remaining torso fell to the ground. He pushed hard on the skull, unable to free it, then jabbed the stick several times but could not pry it from its death hold. He contemplated burying the bones, thinking that animals would drag them off, but then wondered why they'd not been bothered up to now. Finding no identification in the tattered clothes and suspecting the dead man to be the one sluicing on the creek, he wondered if the man had camped nearby.

Shouldering his pack, he began to search and a moment later walked into a small clearing with a partially exposed ring of rocks to contain a fire. A crumpled canvas lay over part of the rocks. As he neared it, he froze in his tracks when he saw the remains of another body lying just beyond the fire-pit. The torso had no head.

Stepping forward, he saw the skull laying against the canvas. Loose dried flesh still clung to a portion of the bone and a short piece of neck bone jutted out from the base. Walking around the head, he noticed the faded red stain that had penetrated the canvas fibers. He believed it to be blood from the man's head when it was separated from the body. But how did it happen, and why hadn't the bones been carried off by animals?

Laying the pack and rifle on the ground, he searched for identification. He found a leather billfold in a pant pocket, and as he slid it out, a gold nugget rolled to the ground. Stephen picked up the nugget to examine it closely, having seen gold on one of his survey jobs northeast of San Francisco. A prospector he'd befriended showed him flakes and nuggets. Stephen reached again into the pocket and pulled out three smaller nuggets, each having a different shape.

Holding the gold tightly in his palm, he opened the billfold for identification. Two papers gave the name Frank Duprey, but no indication of a wife or relative, or where specifically he was from, other than Oregon Territory. Stephen felt sadness that no one knew, or if anyone even cared, that two men had died here.

He looked around for other possessions, spotting the two tattered bedrolls side by side at the edge of the trees. Two broken ropes were tied to trees near each end of the bedrolls. Stephen glanced back to the canvas heaped over the fire-pit that he believed to have been their shelter. A broken rope lay partially hidden beneath it, and he wondered what snapped the ropes, causing the breaks to fray and unravel. Picking up a bedroll and shaking it out, he saw nothing, but a leather pouch fell out of the second bedroll. It contained a few hundred dollars in gold flakes and nuggets. He dropped the other four pieces in the pouch, retied the top and resumed the search.

Finding nothing more, he sat next to his pack and tried to imagine what had happened here, at least a year ago. He wondered if Indians caused the two deaths, or if someone robbed them of their gold, finding a large quantity, and didn't search for the pouch. Stephen could not come to any logical conclusion as to why the head was detached from the body or why the skull of the other man was wedged so tightly in the crotch of a tree. Could the tree grow that much in a year, causing the head to be wedged so tightly? And if so, how did the man get there in the first place?

The more he thought about the strange findings, the more frustrated he became over not knowing what had happened.

Noticing a rifle barrel in the thick grass, he crawled the short distance and grabbed the end of the barrel, but the grass held it tight. As he jerked harder, the grass released its grip and Stephen saw the barrel had been broken, a pronounced bend where it had snapped. He felt through the grass, finding the other end of the barrel with a portion of a broken stalk attached to the breech. He held the two pieces together and saw the obvious bend in the barrel. A tremendous force would have been needed to bend the steel barrel, and even greater to snap it in the middle. Who had strength enough to cause this, he wondered. Let alone place a full-grown man in the crotch of a tree with his head wedged so tight it could not be pried away? There was the snapped rope also, and the head of a man lying several feet from its body. Stephen felt totally mystified as to what could have unleashed such horrible consequences.

Leaning back against his pack, he picked up the pouch of gold, wondering if he should take it or bury it with the remains of the two prospectors? He considered the options: visualizing the burial, placing the gold in the grave, not knowing who to inform of their deaths or, keeping the gold for himself and cashing it out in San Francisco. He decided to keep the gold. After all, what a waste to return it to the earth after the work the two prospectors had done to extract it. Deciding this, he felt obliged to give the men a decent burial.

Near the first body, a large hemlock tree had blown over, tearing the root structure out of the foot of topsoil covering the gravelly bench, leaving a two-foot depression. He would simply have to place the two mens' remains in the hole and knock the clinging soil off the roots.

Completing the task, he decided to camp at the small clearing. He entered the day's experience into his journal, making no speculation as to what happened to the pair of prospectors. He estimated the gold to be two to three hundred dollars in value and lay awake several hours trying to make sense of their death. He thought about the two men working in the creek below and wondered how long it had taken them to recover the small amount he'd found. He also wondered about where they were going, if they had planned to stay here for the winter or go back to one of the Indian villages. Due to their limited supplies he'd seen scattered about, he suspected they would likely go back down the Skeena River to Kuldo or Gitanmaax Village. But then he thought about Bucks Bar and wondered if they may have even planned on travelling there for the winter. Sadly, he folded his journal and lay it on his pack, knowing he would never truly know the answers.

CHAPTER 8

STEPHEN BROKE CAMP AT 7:00, AND LIGHT RAIN STARTED TO FALL AS he left. A few hours later, he deceded the trail toward the Skeena River. He could hear water rushing over rapids as he drew nearer. Suddenly, a hideous scream reverberated up from the river valley, a high-pitched cry from an animal he'd never heard before, different from the one he heard on the coast with Ben and the other wood gatherers. This scream sounded as if something was in pain.

A second outcry echoed up the hillside, then another, lower in tone. Stephen felt drawn to it, wanting to see what made the strange noise. He debated leaving his pack on the trail and hurrying down the hillside or keeping it with him should he need it.

With the pack riding heavy on his shoulders, he cautiously worked his way downhill, angling toward the scream. Slipping occasionally on wet grass and downfall lying along the steep hillside and falling on his rear several times, he felt he made far too much noise. Soon, the river came into view through thick trees and the creature cried out again, but this time it seemed more in anger than pain. Whatever made the noise was near, and he strained to catch sight of it through the leafy vegetation. He moved even slower, not wanting to be heard.

He spotted a criss-cross of dead logs at a bend in the river, tangled into a large log-jam from many years of flooding. This was the place the last cry came from.

Stephen worked his way to the edge of the logs, his loaded rifle ready, his heart pounding at the excitement and fear of not knowing what lay in the midst of the jumbled pile of logs. A deep guttural moan came from the far side of the log-jam where a sandy beach ran beneath the logs. He could see the logs were slick from rain, many of them having had their bark stripped from weathering and from the rushing torrents of water. Wanting to stay on top of the logs in case of a surprise attack, he lowered his pack to the ground and picked his steps carefully. He had a cartridge in the chamber and five in the carbine's tube, feeling this amount of lead would stop any animal.

Nearly to the edge of the log-jam, he stepped slowly and quietly onto one of the higher cross logs. Suddenly his foot slipped off the wet log and he fell backwards, banging the rifle. Landing on his back with the wind nearly knocked from him, the noise of the gun striking wood caused the animal to cry out again, in a different manner, low and menacing, almost evil. Stephen could almost feel the logs vibrate from the sound and he expected some animal to leap over the logs as he lay almost helpless, his back smarting. If he'd lost his grip on the rifle it would have slipped between the logs, perhaps lost for good. Holding the rifle tightly, he waited, but heard no movement.

Quietly, he got to his feet, watching in the direction of the noise. He picked a different spot on the log to place his foot this time, slowly pulling the other leg up, in a squatting position. He saw something hairy lying over the top of the last log in the jam. The top of the log was nearly four feet above the sand bar and the river swept around the bend only a few yards away. He raised higher and pointed the rifle at the hairy mass, trying to decide what it was, when a strong overpowering smell hit him as a slight breeze changed directions. He winced at the pungent odor and squinted his eyes. It smelled much worse than the grizzly sow's strong breath, more like rotting flesh. As he eyed the chunk of hair, he heard a low moan from below it.

Stephen's fear was different from any he'd experienced—the fear of the unknown and, the expectation that any second the unknown would rear up in his face, attacking unmercifully. He crept forward ever so slowly, moving to the side of the mysterious hair mass on the log. Stepping to the second-to-last log, he could see the hair chunk disappear beneath it, draped over the lower log in the other direction toward the ground. The rain had soaked the reddish brown hair and he could see dark coloured flesh beneath it. There seemed to be a knee where it bent over the log.

Stephen swallowed hard. Crouching again he moved one leg onto the last log, then the other. Standing slowly with the rifle pointed and safety off, he saw a giant hairy, two-legged creature on its back, the shoulders and head lying in the sand. Its arms were stretched out to the sides and the eyes were closed. One foot disappeared between the two logs. The free leg was bent at the knee and its foot rested on the side of the log. The huge creature had slipped and jammed a foot into the gap, falling backwards to the sandbar, trapped.

He looked down at the same creature that had awakened him from the terrifying dream in San Francisco. It couldn't be real…it had been a dream! Maybe he was dreaming now? He shut his eyes, squeezed hard, and shook his head slowly, thinking "No…no…it's not real," but the creature remained plainly visible. So he studied the hairy giant carefully.

Its hands were huge, two to three times larger than his own. Barren of hair on the palms, the skin looked dark brown. The arms were nearly six feet in length, almost as long as the legs. He could see toes at the end of the foot pressed against the log and hair hung slightly below the bottom of the foot. Hair covered most of the body, not over an inch long, but not as thick as the hair of the grizzly he saw a few days ago. Its face was nearly barren of hair, showing a large flat nose and narrow lips, and the forehead sloped back toward the top of the head. The scalp hair nearly touched the thick wide eyebrows and the sides of the head were covered with long sparse hair. Could this thing be part human or part gorilla, an animal he'd seen at a sideshow on the San Francisco wharf? Just what the heck is this thing, he wondered.

Suddenly the eyes opened, looking up at the sky. Stephen moved his rifle preparing to shoot if it tried to reach him. The beast heard the noise and looked up. Its small dark, piercing eyes gazed directly into Stephen's, their fixed look lasting several seconds. The giant creature pulled its arms to the sides and raised its shoulders off the sand, screaming out as pressure pulled against the trapped leg. It stretched one of the long arms to the top of the log and tried pulling itself up, but the large hand slipped off the wet log, leaving scratch marks from the hard, flat, dark-coloured finger nails.

Stephen could see the giant was trapped for certain and either its foot or leg had to be broken to cause the amount of pain it was obviously suffering. The giant moaned again, and the shoulders lay back to the ground. Stephen felt compassion for the injured animal, if indeed it was an animal and not some sort of man-creature. He wondered now if he could shoot if he had to, then remembered he'd shot a man just a few weeks ago to save his own life.

He also wondered how he could help free the creature from the near certain death trap. There were no branches on the smooth log for it to grab hold and pull itself upright. Unless there was another of its kind nearby to lift the trapped mate, it appeared there was no way to get the creature free.

Looking at the trapped foot, Stephen took a deep breath. What could he do? The logs were three to four feet in diameter and with the small hatchet, it would take days to chop through.

The eight inch gap between the logs gave Stephen an idea. If he could find the right piece of wood, he might be able to help. The giant made another attempt to free itself, causing another outcry of pain.

Stephen made his way back over the log-jam to his pack and pulled out the hatchet. Feeling safe for the moment, he leaned his rifle against the pack, then looked for a small tree of the right size and shape.

A half hour later he found what he looked for, halfway up the steep hillside. He cut down the ten-inch tree in two minutes, hacking at each side. As it fell, the top caught in branches of another and hung up solidly. He pushed the tree back and forth, but the medium size hemlock wouldn't budge, the base still clinging to the cut stump by the inner wood fibers. Chopping the remainder and kicking the tree off the stump, the top barely moved. He thought he would have to cut it through again, but after shaking and pushing several times, the tree slowly rolled to the side. He kicked it a few more times to help work its way to the ground, relieved when it fell with a thud.

A few feet up, the tree began a gentle curve, and at twelve feet the tree forked. He cut through it again a foot above the fork; each forked branch having a five-inch diameter. Stephen hoped that when used for leverage, it would hold the weight of the beast, which must have weighed seven hundred pounds.

By the time he dragged the cut tree to the bottom of the hill, his clothes were soaked from wet brush and from sweat of the exertion of climbing, chopping, pushing and finally dragging the tree downhill. He pulled the tree over the top of the log-jam, laying it down before coming into view of the hairy beast. The giant heard the noise, but lay still, looking up at where it had last seen the strange creature on the log above.

Stephen retrieved his rifle, hoping not to have to use it. Picking his way over the slick logs, he appeared above the helpless giant, causing the creature to struggle and cry out again. He raised the rifle in the air for the beast to see and hoping it somehow understood his meaning, he laid the rifle down, then stood up again, showing the rifle gone. The creature watched the display, lying still with outstretched arms.

Stephen picked up the large end of the cut tree, worked it onto the higher log, then pulled it around parallel to where the fork was near the beast's injured leg. While trying to keep balance on the slick wet logs and raising the larger end, he worked the fork into the gap and raised it to an upright position, grunting with exertion at the heavy weight. The beast struggled to free itself, fearing the raised log was meant for harm.

Stephen winced at the loud shrieks of pain, watching carefully that it didn't reach a long arm up to his leg, to pull him off the logs. He could only imagine what this giant would do to him.

Suddenly his thoughts returned to the two prospectors he'd buried. His mind raced, envisioning the beast picking up the first man and slamming his head into the tree crotch, pulling the head right off the second man, snapping the ropes on the shelter and bending the rifle barrel with its powerful hands. Is it possible that's what happened to the two men? Did this same creature attack them with no warning? Stephen had second thoughts about freeing this possible man-killer. What would the giant do to him when loose? Looking at the rifle, he wondered just how many bullets it would take to stop this enormous creature.

He also thought about the story the fishing guide told him at the camp-fire, about a giant manlike beast with reddish brown hair and a terrible stench. He'd laughed at the possibility then, but as he looked at the struggling animal, he was far from laughter. This creature looked just as the man described. And, there was the Indians stories of Bukwas, the hairy giants who carried off women and children.

"*I don't believe it!*" he said. "The stories *are* real." He shook his head slowly, astonished that it lay trapped before him.

The creature stopped struggling, and with compassion returning to Stephen, he held out a hand with the palm toward the beast and rocked his arm up and down to portray a comforting motion, hoping the creature would understand. Then he returned to the task, working the forked end of the tree further into the gap. Stephen lowered the large end of the tree toward the beast until he could no longer hold the weight and let it drop. The giant flinched and tried to deflect the falling log, but when it reached the binding point, the log was slightly to the side of the beast and four feet above its waist.

Realizing the purpose of the log, the creature reached out a long arm and grabbed hold, causing the tree to bend from the weight. Stephen didn't know what to expect, so he picked up the rifle and moved aside.

The giant lifted its weight off the ground, then in a surprisingly quick motion pushed upward, and pulled itself to the top of the large log, crying out. It angled the trapped foot sideways and pulled free, then moaned gutturally, looking at the ankle, perhaps trying to determine the reason for the pain.

Only a short distance from Stephen when the beast stood erect, it rose to eight feet in height, and the tremendous size took Stephen's breath. He dared not move.

The creature tested the foot, applying pressure, and pulled up in pain. The giant sat on the log with its legs hanging over the edge, then turned its upper body toward Stephen, their eyes meeting. Stephen could plainly see another of the giant's features: the head sat squarely on the shoulders, there was no neck.

The small, deep-set dark eyes showed no fear or anger, and Stephen sensed a hint of thankfulness as he stared into them. The eyes did not seem to blink like a human's, but remained open much like a dog's eyes did when staring at you. The creature pursed its mouth and made a soft squeaky noise, like the meow of a kitten. Stephen had the strong feeling it had just thanked him.

Then the beast pushed off the log and crumbled to the ground, emitting a loud shriek from the injured leg.

Stephen felt certain the leg was broken and wondered how the animal would survive, particularly if it depended on meat to subsist. The beast lifted the injured leg and probed its ankle.

Stephen thought about what he could he do to help. Put the crippled giant out of its misery by shooting it? After all, that's what they did with horses or cattle and even dogs. But this is a wild creature, and if unable to find food it would die a slow, agonizing death. Stephen found difficulty visualizing the starving animal struggling to survive, but how else could he help? What could he do that would give the giant a chance to live? His mind seemed blank, nothing coming to him.

He moved toward the fulcrum used to free the beast, looking at the gap and the fork wedged between the logs, when suddenly he had a far-fetched idea.

Stephen set the rifle down and tried lifting the tree, but the large butt end proved too heavy. He tried again, but it didn't budge. The giant sat motionless, watching the effort.

Retrieving the hatchet from the pack, Stephen looked down at the hairy creature, estimating the height to cut the log, then chopped it off several feet from the fork. He pulled the end from between the logs and stood the cut piece upright, the fork at the top of his head, thinking it should be the right height. He lowered the cut end to the sand bar and tipped the fork toward the beast's side. The creature raised an arm to deflect the fall, but the wooden piece landed alongside.

Stephen hoped the creature would know what to do next, but it merely picked the wood up in one hand like a large club and studied it. Stephen looked across the log-jam and spotted several dead branches sticking upright above the pile. He picked his way across the rain-soaked logs and found one with a forked branch, smaller, but it looked nearly like the one he'd cast down to the giant. Returning, he measured the height and chopped it off. Holding the branch toward the creature, making sure it watched this intricate procedure, he placed the fork under an arm and, putting weight on it, lifted his leg as if it were injured.

Stephen took an explanatory step, using the branch as a crutch. He looked at the creature and took another step, then another, but the crutch slipped on the wet log. Before he knew what had happened, he lay flat on his back on the sandbar at the feet of the hairy giant.

He scrambled to get to his feet and get away from the killer beast, but fell backwards against the log. Now Stephen was the one trapped. The giant need only lean forward a few feet, reach out with those long arms and grab his face with its huge powerful hands, just like in his nightmare back home. Fear filled his entire being; he was certain the creature would grab him.

The beast started to rock back and forth. Was aggression mounting? Was the beast getting ready to attack? Stephen thought of closing his eyes, not wanting to see what would come next. The creature's stench alone made him want to close his eyes, as he scrunched his face and held his breath.

Then the beast opened its mouth slightly, revealing almost human-like teeth, worn and badly stained. There were no fangs like one would expect a wild beast to have, only larger teeth than normal. The bottom of its feet pointed directly toward Stephen, twice the size of his jack boots.

The giant lifted a hand off the ground and let it fall back to the sand, it's teeth were still showing and it's upper body still rocking. Stephen wondered what the actions meant and the thought came to him. "Is this thing laughing at me?" It repeated the hand movement and Stephen spoke out loud, "The damn thing is laughing at me! It could have killed me and eaten me by now, and all the stupid thing wants to do is laugh at me. I'll be damned." he said, shaking his head. "Nobody is going to believe this. I fall on my butt next to a stinking, wild, hairy, half-man, half-ape giant …and the stupid thing sits here laughing. I don't believe it."

Hearing the garbled sounds from this small, strange looking thing, the giant stopped rocking, closed its mouth and looked into Stephen's eyes again. "Oops!", Stephen said aloud, thinking he shouldn't have spouted off. Maybe the human language angered it. The creature turned to the side and lifted upright with ease, keeping weight off the foot. The giant then leaned down and picked up the makeshift crutch. With its back toward Stephen, the large creature placed a hand on top of the fork, and stood motionless. Was it thinking of what to do with the forked stick, perhaps remembering what Stephen had done?

Stephen slowly crawled away from the log, grasped his example of a crutch, rose and began to move quietly off to the side of the giant. It towered over his 6'1" height; the upper body was massive, the chest half as thick as it was wide. The upper arms were nearly a foot in diameter, and the end of the fingers hung just below the knees. He clearly noticed the cone shape of the head sloping back to a higher point on top. No ears were visible, hidden beneath the longer hair.

Being less concerned now about the creature harming him, he moved into view, staying several feet to the side. The creature turned its upper body, looking down at him. Stephen lifted the crutch again and slowly placed it under his arm, then hobbled in front of the beast.

Then it happened. The giant placed the fork under its arm and leaned weight on the crude crutch. Stephen smiled, nodding in approval and said, "Yes, that's it fellow. Now walk." And Stephen demonstrated again how to walk with the crutch. The giant took a single step and the injured foot touched the ground, causing a groan. Then, it tried another step without touching. Then another.

The mysterious hairy creature hobbled across the short sandy beach and through a stretch of small, rounded river rock. Stephen noticed the giant's imprints across the sand and where it stepped into a piece of mud, leaving deep impressions from the tremendous weight. The five toes showed well in the mud, even the small ridges in the skin were visible.

At the edge of the brush, the giant stopped and faced Stephen. Stephen gave a short salute and wave, and said, "So long, you big, smelly bugger." The hairy, reddish-brown giant turned and hobbled into the bush.

CHAPTER 9

IT HAD BEEN THREE DAYS SINCE STEPHEN'S ENCOUNTER WITH WHAT he finally admitted was a Bukwas, the legendary hairy giant devil that ate women and children. He convinced himself the creature was no devil and it didn't eat humans. He knew it had intelligence, more so than any other animal. He had entered the encounter in his journal, but the more he read it over, the more he wished he hadn't. No one would believe him. They'd say he got into strange wild mushrooms up there in the woods of Canada, which made him mad, made him hallucinate.

Stephen thought of the wild mushrooms because of the experience of just a day ago. He had eaten wild mushrooms in California, watching as Hugh picked them. Hugh showed him what to look for in edible mushrooms, so here in the far northern climate, Stephen tried to remember the brief instructions.

He couldn't believe the numerous varieties and shapes of mushrooms and fungus he saw during September—dome shaped, dish shaped, cone shaped, round, oval, nearly square, short, fat, skinny and tall; colours of green, red, pale, pink, purple, brown, gray, white and nearly black. He didn't know the name of any of them but found two different types that were the right shapes on top and in the veil underneath, so he picked two. He ate one the first night, fried in eulachon oil, with boiled rice, smoked salmon and a pinch of salt on the mushroom pieces.

The next evening, he ate the second mushroom raw, with beans, hard-tack and dried caribou meat he'd boiled. An hour later he began feeling lightheaded, as he had when he tipped too many whiskey glasses in the Seattle saloon. He saw coloured lights floating around the campfire and audibly described them to whoever might listen. He crawled out of his bedroll, stripped off his underwear and danced barefoot around the campfire, trying to catch the pretty lights.

The next morning he felt groggy, remembering only the lights while lying in his bedroll. His naked body was covered with mosquito bites and his underwear lay on the damp ground. He vowed to never eat mushrooms again from the dense forests of this northern British Columbia Colony.

Stephen took astronomic observations on cloudless periods every few days and made good progress determining a route. He kept the survey instruments wiped clean of moisture that collected while wrapped inside the backpack, for even though days were warm, the nights were cool and heavy with dew. He cleaned his rifle nearly every day. If he let it go, it might misfire when critically needed.

Stephen descended to the Skeena River occasionally for fresh water, a bath, or washing of soiled clothes. The glacial fed waters were cold, taking his breath away when he either jumped in the river naked or washed at the small creeks. It rejuvenated his spirits, causing him to sing aloud as he walked on, talking to himself on occasion, often using different accents as a means of entertainment and practice. He even answered himself sometimes, but in another accent, as if two companions of different nationalities were travelling, remarking on the different sights observed.

Stephen bagged four blue grouse in a three day period. Two were shot with his rifle, aiming at their heads at close range. The other two were shot with the pistol, but not being as accurate, he nearly ruined the breast of one and the legs of another. He savored the caribou jerky he'd traded for, wondering what the animal looked like.

He'd seen several black bears as he walked, all running away, likely never having seen a man before. Moose were scarce; he saw an occasional track or droppings and the occasional tracks of another hoofed animal, smaller than a moose but larger than deer. Those tracks seemed to head either straight down toward the Skeena or straight up the steep hill to the west toward the higher mountain peaks in the distance. He hoped to see one of the animals, but the scarcity of tracks made it unlikely.

A variety of birds flourished during the summer months, and it came as a surprise to see robins, canaries, hummingbirds and even bluebirds in open areas and swallows near the river. White gulls frequented the river, as did the magnificent bald eagle. Whenever he stopped to rest, he took pleasure in the chirps, peeps, whistles and squawks, the only sounds in the forest. Small chickadees would flit to a branch nearby to investigate this new creature in the woods, and Stephen made soft clucks with his tongue, bringing them within five feet. Ravens were practically everywhere he travelled, their black feathers making them easy to spot, even in the heavy foliage of tree tops where they perched to squawk their warning of the new intruder.

Stephen averaged ten miles a day, taking time for map details and readings. He continued side excursions to gain vantage points for better route locations and landmark identification, when low lying clouds didn't obstruct the view.

The trail became steeper, and when it split off, he remembered the map Kwabellem had made and followed the most westerly trail, the other continuing up the Skeena. Snow had fallen on higher mountain peaks during a three-day rain, which eventually soaked through his oilskins. It was nearly impossible to dry wet clothes unless he found a large heavy-limbed coniferous tree that little rain penetrated through, where he hung his clothes next to a well-banked fire. His feet became sore from the wet jackboots, and skin peeled away in small chunks. Cracked skin between his toes were particularly painful and he dreaded putting on damp socks in the mornings, pulling his wet boots over them.

The morning the rain stopped, he'd camped at the divide between the Skeena and Nass River watersheds. He had coughed during the night and couldn't keep warm in the damp bedroll. When he awoke, his head ached, his tonsils were swollen and sore and his skin burned up, yet he continued to shiver. He knew he'd go no further that day, having had colds with a fever many times before, keeping him in bed four to five days.

Struggling out of the bedroll, he retrieved the water bag, then dug into his pack to find the tin of medical supplies. Pulling the small vial from the tin, he took two tablets of an analgesic, Antipyrene, obtained from a doctor in San Francisco, he told Stephen it should help with flu symptoms as well and headaches.

He became concerned about water, having only two quarts in the canvas bag. The nearest water was a lake, four miles back down the trail.

Stephen had always had someone to help when he turned this ill: someone who took care of meals, water, and the few medicines available, mostly home remedies. His mother cared for him when younger, his sister and father later on, then Rachel. He thought of Rachel as he lay in the cold bedroll, wishing she was here now, or better yet, he was at their home with her there to care for him. He missed her terribly as memories danced through his head, until he drifted off to sleep with the warm, welcome sunshine driving away the cold chill.

Stephen slept most of the day, waking a few times, coughing. He knew he needed to dry his damp bedroll, try to eat and make something warm to drink. Weak, he forced himself to dress and look for dry firewood. When the fire blazed, he spread the bedroll over nearby bushes where remaining sunlight and heat from the fire would dry it. Heating water for tea, he noticed only a quart of the precious liquid remained. He nibbled on smoked salmon and sipped hot tea. Two dark blue Steller's jays squawked nearby, hoping he would leave a morsel on the ground. A raven gronked along the timber-covered ridge line, and a cool breeze swept down from the snow-covered peaks. He had nothing warm to put around him and felt sad and lonely, shivering by the fire. Finally he crawled into his still damp, cold bedroll and fell asleep within an hour.

The fever broke three days later. He hadn't had water for over a day, and he continued to cough, nearly vomiting when the coughs were strongest. A croup is what his mother had called it. She'd placed hot mustard packs on his chest, getting him up each day to breathe steam from hot herb treated water with a blanket over his head, hoping to break the chest cold. He knew he would have to suffer this cold further, probably several more days if he could keep dry.

But he needed water and debated if he should return to the lake or continue northward in hopes of finding a small creek. Having lost several days on the trail, he hoped they would not be crucial to completing his task. From what Kwabellem had told him, he was now nearly halfway to Buck's Bar.

He decided to press on, remembering the many small creeks he'd crossed so far, and he felt certain he would not have to walk more than a day to find water. His feet had healed considerably during the illness, and if the rain would just hold off for a while, he believed his croup would soon subside. The brisk nights caused leaves of poplar trees and a few bushes to turn yellow. He knew it would only turn colder as he travelled.

The bedroll and supplies were pushed tightly in the pack and ready to shoulder by 9:00 a.m. Stephen had trouble getting the pack on in his weakened state. Walking the trail, he broke into a sweat, the constant cough creating extreme headaches. Grateful to be going downhill, he still needed to rest often. Six hours and five miles down the trail, he came to a small trickling flow of clear water. He'd decided the first good water he came to would be camp for the night.

It was one of his rougher camps with no flat area to pitch a lean-to. Stephen had to place his bedroll so his feet were against the base of a large hemlock tree, and he awoke several times during the night to straighten his bent knees and push back uphill.

Again he left camp late in the morning, having to stop for frequent rests, but made seven miles. He struggled to keep on, with the sweats, coughing and headaches, feeling obligated to complete the survey and get the results to the telegraph company.

Stephen had travelled along the east side of the Nass River, and the camp at the end of the week was near the head of the Klappan River[11]. Effects from flu symptoms subsided after a few days and his strength returned, but the food supply was dangerously low. Checking supplies that night, he found one piece of smoked salmon, one of caribou, a cup of flour, and a half cup each of rice and beans. He could stretch this for three days but estimated he needed eight to ten to reach Buck's Bar. He would have to find wild game.

Late afternoon of the following day, he saw the tops of brush moving next to a pine tree. He slipped the pack off and crept closer, cautious that it might be a bear. Then he saw the head of an animal as it climbed the brush to get to the leaves. Realizing what he'd found, he was disappointed, not wanting to eat a porcupine to survive. The notion of an animal having hundreds of sharp quills on the outside caused concern regarding the meat on the inside. Who would want to eat a pin cushion, he thought. But the more he watched, and not having approached other game, the more he thought he should take the offering presented to him.

Skinning the animal carefully, he was aware that a careless touch of a needle sharp quill would result in it driving deep into his skin. Roasting the meat over an open fire, he saved one of the legs for the next day and took a small bite from the other, testing to see if it tasted of pine bark. He'd seen a number of pine trees girdled by the mostly nocturnal animal and believed the bark to be its main diet.

Surprisingly, the meat tasted sweet, but was stringy. He gnawed the leg bone clean, then dug into the meat along the back, followed by the small front legs. Satisfied, he wiped the grease from his lips with the back of his hand, then wiped the hand on his pant leg. His beard had small particles of meat scattered in the now long hair, and water trickled down his chest as he swallowed from the canvas water bag. Besides the grouse, salmon, and ground squirrel, this was the freshest meat he'd eaten since the deer meat back on the *Mumford*. However, he longed for mashed potatoes with gravy and hot apple pie with thick brown crust.

Lying in his bedroll with the fire flickering, the silence was interrupted by the ghostly howl of a wolf down the Klappan River Valley. This was the second wolf he'd heard since leaving Kuldo; this one much closer than the first. He'd been hoping to see wolves, curious about their size after seeing the tracks in the sand where the Kuldo River ran into the Skeena. Then came a second, different howl, higher up the hillside on the east side of the valley, followed by several more of the incredibly eerie calls, causing him to pull the rifle closer before drifting off to sleep.

Making good time along the well-worn trail on the east side of the Klappan Valley, he came to an old burn. Numerous dead snags stood about like sentinel's watching over the otherwise treeless landscape. Small, waist-high bushes grew abundantly and he noticed some were berry laden, so stopped to test them. The one he liked best was the huckleberries, and he took time to gather some in a small cooking pot. When it was nearly full, he worked his way back down the slope toward the pack on the trail.

As he stepped onto the trail a large grey wolf stood on the upper side of his pack, twenty feet away, its neck stretched, sniffing the strange scents. Stephen froze, realizing he'd left the rifle leaning against his pack, and the pistol was inside. He cursed at himself for this mistake.

The wolf stood motionless, yellow eyes staring intensely at him. Stephen vacillated about what to do, the stare-down continuing. Then its upper lip curled as the wolf bared large menacing teeth, and a low guttural growl caused a chill to run through Stephen's entire body. The thought of those long white fangs ripping into flesh was terrifying. He knew *this* animal was *definitely* a meat eater.

He'd heard stories of wolf packs attacking cattle in California, their ferocious ripping and tearing of live flesh was a horrible sight. The wolves didn't stop their attack when cattlemen fired their rifle into the pack, not until several had been wounded and yelped loudly, causing others to release their prey and reluctantly leave.

Suddenly, another menacing growl came from behind him, and fear shot through his mind. Instinctively, he knew if he turned to look at the one behind, the big grey would attack. He felt only seconds remained before the one behind would lunge at a leg, sinking its strong sharp fangs deep into his flesh. If that happened, the other wolf would be on him in seconds, and he knew he would be torn to shreds. He had to act!

Throwing the pot of blueberries at the grey wolf and yelling a long loud, "Haaaaaaa!" while running swiftly toward it, he hoped to scare it back before the other wolf mounted an attack. The flying pot and scattering berries worked, causing the grey wolf to jump aside. Stephen's eyes fastened on the rifle leaning against the downhill side of the pack by a clump of alders. It held a shell in the chamber, as it had done since the grizzly encounter. Grabbing the rifle, he hoped the grey wolf was too startled to attack immediately, and swung swiftly to face the second wolf, slipping the safety ahead with his thumb.

The black wolf was fully off the ground in a leap, having run after Stephen when he broke for the rifle. Stephen fell backwards anticipating the wolf's momentum, and before its chest touched the barrel of the rifle, he pulled the trigger.

The impact of the 140-pound wolf proved tremendous, the rifle barrel taking most of the weight, the gun stock jamming into Stephen's side, breaking a rib just above the stomach. The wolf fell against the pack, jarring it away from the alders, causing the wolf and pack to roll across Stephen's waist. The dying wolf began a violent rabbit kick with its hind feet, tearing the pack's canvas cover with its sharp claws.

Stephen rolled to his right, trying to sit up, but stopped short, the pain from the broken rib sharp. Hearing the wolf kicking, he thought it would attack again and quickly jacked another round in the chamber. He turned in time to see the grey wolf moving in, and a second later, its sharp teeth sank into Stephen's left calf. He cried out and his body stiffened. He rammed the gun barrel into the wolf's neck and fired. The leg flesh ripped as the impact knocked the wolf back and it lay limp while its fallen companion delivered its final death kicks. Hearing another wolf running through the brush, he urgently worked another round in the chamber and fired in the air, frightening off two more wolves.

Except for his heavy breathing, there was total silence. He lay back, reliving the ordeal, while his heart pounded in his ears. A moment later, he explored his injuries, gingerly probing the rib with a finger, then sitting upright to examine the leg wound. He was more concerned about the damage there. He slowly pulled up the pant leg to reveal blood trickling down the skin. Two puncture wounds in the shin had struck bone and were tender to the touch. He turned the leg to see the ripped calf muscle and the wound discharging dark red. He had to get the bleeding stopped.

Pulling the pack closer, he found the medical tin and took out the roll of gauze and a small bottle of iodine. Taking off his leather belt, he wrapped it twice around the injured leg, three inches above the wound, then buckled it. Finding a stout stick beneath the alders, he broke off a short piece and placed the stick in the loop, twisting the belt tight to stop the bleeding. He pulled a shirt from the pack and using water from the canvas bag, wiped the blood away from the wounds.

After cleaning, he poured the iodine into the deep fang wounds, stiffening from the burning pain, fanning the wound with his hat, wishing he hadn't put so much on. After dabbing iodine on the shin wounds, he placed a small wad of gauze on each fang-torn hole, then wrapped the gauze tightly around the calf, and pulled the pant down to the tourniquet. Slowly getting to his feet, he looked at the dead wolves and thought to himself that he just wanted to *see* wolves, not to have to fight for his life with them.

He thought of how close he'd come to death once again, but this time it was a fight for his life rather than the fright of his life that the grizzly had left him with. He shook his head, remembering how he'd thought this would be any easy trip.

Stephen tried walking on the injured leg, but found it too painful. Sitting on the pack to think, he loosened the tourniquet for a short time and re-tightened it, watching the gauze turn red. He wouldn't be able to walk on the leg for a few days and considered making camp here. He could try wolf meat for food and his water bag was nearly full, or he could make himself a crutch like he'd done for the Bukwas giant.

Looking into the small clump of alders, he saw a branch with a fork that would suffice as a crutch until he got out of the burned area and found a more sturdy one. Chopping the branch with the hatchet, he wrapped the bloody shirt around the fork for padding, and tested it out.

Before shouldering the pack, he decided to eat one of those danged wolves that tried to eat him. Skinning a back leg of the gray wolf, he cut out a hunk of meat, wrapped it in his last shirt, and placed it in the pack.

He found the broken rib too painful to shoulder the pack as usual, so set it on the uphill side of the trail and slid beneath the shoulder straps. With great difficulty, he lifted the entire weight with one leg, pushing himself up with the crutch. Picking up his rifle, he hobbled slowly down the valley trail.

CHAPTER 10

STEPHEN WALKED WITHOUT USE OF A CRUTCH WITHIN THREE DAYS, but limped with considerable pain. A few days later he came to the camp of nine Tsetsaut Indians, hunting and gathering berries. Two of the natives spoke enough English to talk with Stephen, and he learned they were called the Long Grass of the Sekani. One of the two was a plump woman named Chehela, who belonged to the Wolf phratry of the Kispiox people. A phratry, comprised several totemic clans. She'd been given in marriage by her father at age 15, and had come to the Long Grass people by the same trail as Stephen travelled. Hearing this prompted Stephen to ask if she'd ever seen Bukwas, and the idle talk nearby ceased when they heard the name.

"Why you ask of Bukwas?" the man named Kolaylli said. "Among our people, we no talk of Bukwas.

"Sorry," Stephen said. "I heard the name from a man back on the coast. I was just curious about it."

"Bukwas bad...devil. We not speak of him no more."

Perplexed regarding the natives' reluctance to talk about the giant hairy creature, Stephen thought their Bukwas might be something different from the one he'd encountered. He knew the Bukwas to be an intelligent animal or human or whatever, but yet there remained the mystery of the two dead miners. After all, he thought, these people live in this country and seem to fear the creature, while I, having only a single encounter, am only passing through. But the encounter was unlike any other.

The natives informed Stephen of a shorter route to Buck's Bar than by following the Klappan to the Stikine River and then traversing downstream. There would be another trail five miles further on, turning west along a small stream to the Stikine, only a few miles below Buck's Bar. It would save two days' walking. Stephen hoped the route would be adequate for the telegraph line.

They asked why he limped, if he'd been shot by the white man's gun? He told them about the wolf attack, and they seemed to hold him in higher esteem after he showed the leg wound and pointed out the broken rib.

All were interested in the story, except for the woman of the wolf clan who disapproved of killing wolves.

They invited Stephen to stay the night, but were surprised when he had little food to contribute to the evening meal. He still had wolf meat in his pack but for Chehela's sake, did not offer it.

The meal consisted of skinned gutted ground hogs and grouse, mixed with a great variety of roots and wild onions then boiled in a hand-woven basket that became waterproof when soaked. Placing the basket near the fire, heated rocks rinsed of ashes carried with split-wood tongs were lowered into the partially filled basket. When the water finally boiled, they added the food, then covered the top with a mat. Rocks were replaced with additional heated ones until the food became fully cooked. Stephen found the hot stew delicious, and it was a pleasant treat to talk with someone again, even though it was difficult to get correct interpretations. He entertained the group with several different accents, and even those who didn't understand the words were amused at the different sounds they had never heard before .

The Long Grass people, he learned, were somewhat nomadic, travelling to different parts of their territory. Everything depended on the gathering of food, not only for immediate needs but also in preparation for the long cold winter. Forty and fifty below weather was not uncommon for at least two weeks during mid-winter. Even though the Sekani spent the winter in the lower elevation of the Klappan, five feet of snow was not uncommon. They were literally housebound for up to two months.

Life was difficult and although they had not been ravaged by smallpox as some bands had, their numbers seemed to stay nearly the same. They lived nearly the identical existence as their people had for several thousand years. In a way, Stephen felt sorry for them, who had never known anything different. He couldn't imagine himself having to live their way of life—never knowing the simple pleasure of eating a fine dinner at the Comstock, taking a train ride across the plains or sending a telegram to a sister in Seattle. But as he lay in his bed that night thinking about the evening with them, he couldn't help but notice how content this small group of people were. Each person had contributed something toward the evening meal. Be it preparing the meat, the roots and onions, hauling water for the basket, packing in firewood, breaking the wood pieces with a large stone hammer, starting the fire with a flint spark, or making a latrine—everyone had helped. They laughed a great deal and seemed to kid one another often, but yet seemed to have great respect for each other. Stephen realized that had he been born into their world, he would be the same. It wouldn't matter if he ever saw a fancy meal on a dinner plate or ever boarded a train. It certainly wouldn't matter if he couldn't pay money to send a telegram to someone and never know if they received it. He would just be like they were. Peaceful, happy, struggling to survive. Never knowing anything different—and not caring about it one way or the other. He had obtained a new outlook on these native people who lived off the land.

The following morning, the friendly natives gave Stephen extra food, and he expressed gratitude for their hospitality, then continued along the trail. He still limped from the leg wound but was in less pain now, and the cracked rib continued to bother him. He had to treat it gingerly. Six days later, Stephen arrived at the Stikine, then followed the trail upriver until he saw the buildings of Buck's Bar on the steep hillside across the river. A cable car strung across the river was a welcome sight, and several minutes later, he stepped on the opposite bank, then walked toward the group of men washing gold further upstream.

The small town had once reeled with excitement when several thousand gold miners milled about, seeking out their fortunes. Now, a dozen miners were all that remained in Buck's Bar.

Approaching the first group of men, they stopped work and watched the newcomer limp toward them."Hello there." Stephen said to the four miners. "How you fellows doing? Been a while since I've seen a white man. Stephen Doyle's the name." He extended a hand toward one of the bearded men wearing a wide brim hat. "I'm with the Western Union Telegraph Company, surveying a route from down by Kispiox Village."

The bearded man said, "Must be a bunch of you surveyors lookin' fer that route, mister. You're the third one this year."

Stephen recalled his meeting with Conway, who had mentioned sending others out on different routes. "How long since they were here?" Stephen asked.

"Well, let's see now," the man wearing the hat said, rubbing his chin and turning to the others. "When did those first two guys show up?"

"About April," the man leaning on his shovel answered. "Ice wasn't out of the river yet. Around the middle of April, I think."

"Yeah, that's about right," a man with thick red hair chipped in. "They came from the south, too. Said their route wasn't too good. It was only a week or so later when that guy named Pope showed up from a different direction. Came down the Stikine with three Indians and three dogs. A few days later, the first two guys headed back south, looking for a better route. Pope stayed several days and built a boat out of old sluice boxes and abandoned houses. When the ice went out, floated right on outta' here."

"I guess his route didn't work out either," Stephen said. "I came up the Skeena and crossed over to the head of the Nass, then down the Klappan. The route there looks pretty good."

"How come you ain't got nobody with you?" The first man asked. "Ain't too smart to be traipsing around this country by yourself. Besides, we heard three men were supposed to be arriving here about now."

Three men, Stephen wondered, then remembered Ryan Evers, the man who'd murdered Jock. Evers mentioned he'd seen young Morison and told him that he, was supposed to catch up to the surveyors to help them. But how did these men know?

"I...ah, had a partner," Stephen answered, wondering if he should give details of the murder, then decided not to. "He had an accident way down on the Skeena and couldn't go any further. Took the river back down. Don't know anything about a third man though.

"I was going to hire an Indian guide in Kispiox, but the only one I came across who spoke English didn't seem reliable. When I got to Kuldo Village, the men who knew the area best were off hunting, so I found out what I could about the trails and just plodded on. Some natives camped back on the Klappan told me of a shorter route. Saved me a couple of days."

"Which way you going back?" the redhead asked.

"I'll go back the same way. I've a few more observations to take and some fill-in to do on my map."

"Well, if you're in need of provisions, a young fellow named Morison and a guy named Brown were here just a week ago. Came upriver with a crew of natives and sixty foot canoes. Left a bunch of food rations for you and any other explorers that might be coming up. He's the one that told us three surveyors would be showing up here soon."

Surprised to hear Morison's name again, Stephen thought of how he'd last seen him guarding supplies destined for Kispiox, the day before Jock's murder. So, Morison did remember the man in the buckskin jacket, but Stephen wondered why Morison had told them three surveyors instead of two—unless Evers didn't return to Morison's camp. Perhaps that's what happened, but where was Evers now?

"I'm glad to hear he brought supplies." Stephen said. "I'm right out of grub. Thought I'd buy some here at your trading post."

The men laughed while the one leaning on his shovel responded. "Tradin' post. There sure in hell ain't no tradin' post here, sonny. Hasn't been for two years. We gotta' go downriver for tradin' and get our own staples down there. Got a man out huntin' every day. Woulda' had damn little to give you, so you're real lucky Morison came along."

Stephen forced a smile, thinking himself fortunate in his timing. If he'd not had those delays along the trip, he would have arrived before Morison, starting back with little or no food. "Yeah, guess I am pretty lucky."

"Stay a day or two, mister," the redhead said. "You probably need the rest. We've enough extra for a few meals." He told Stephen which cabin was theirs and where he could find the cached rations, and said they'd be there around 7:00. Stephen thanked them and turned toward the buildings.

He entered what remained of the once bustling, short-lived town, most shacks having been abandoned two years earlier and had crumbled from winter snows or torn down for Pope's boat. Most cabins had been hastily constructed in the early stages of the 1862 gold rush, and building materials were of poor quality, being cut and sawed on site. Buck's Bar was renamed Telegraph Creek when Alexandre (Buck) Choquette, the man who'd discovered gold here, met Morison and Brown further down the Stikine River while he searched for gold with his Indian wife. Buck Choquette had questioned them regarding the amount of supplies the large Indian canoes were carrying, and when informed supplies were for the telegraph line explorers and construction workers, he told Morison, "Well then, we should call it Telegraph Creek from now on instead of Buck's Bar.

Heck sakes, I don't need my name on it any more. All the gold's been mined out anyway."

While waiting for the four miners to return, Stephen aired out his bedroll, washed his clothes and took a cold swim in a calm back eddy of the green-coloured water of the Stikine River.

Before supper, the redhead, Alex Peterson, handed Stephen a whiskey bottle and tin cup. Stephen hesitated, remembering the last time he took a drink, but the memory quickly subsided, as he felt a strong need. Pouring a half cup, he voiced his surprise at their having whiskey way up here, and one man said it was one of their main staples. Kept them going. They joined Stephen in their ritual drink before supper.

By the time one of the men cooked the evening meal, Stephen's words started to slur slightly and subsided completely after eating when he dozed in the corner of the shack with his back against the wall. He awoke with Alex nudging a foot with the toe of his boot saying, "Come on, Doyle, let's get you settled in that shack with your supplies. You can sleep in late as you want."

Stephen slept until noon, surprising himself, as he'd not done that for many years. Stepping out the door of the shack was a total surprise; an inch of snow lay on the ground and was still falling. He hurried to the river, retrieving the washed clothes off the willows. Returning to the miners' shack, he rekindled the cook stove fire and placed his clothes around the shack to dry. He decided to begin the return trek in the morning before snow became a problem. He selected provisions from the boxes of food rations Morison left. Fortunately, there were additional matches in waterproof containers packed in each box, as he'd exhausted his supply. Before the miners returned, Stephen's dry clothes and provisions were packed, ready to leave at first light.

He wanted to average twenty miles a day, to include additional astronomic readings and map completions in order to reach Kispiox around the third week of October. This would be a week later than Conway thought the construction of the telegraph line should reach the village. He needed to put in some long days.

Stephen ate breakfast with the four miners and went with them to the river. The snow continued falling as he shook hands and wished them luck on their prospecting, telling them to look him up in San Francisco if they ever get down that way. They watched Stephen cross the Stikine on the cable car and look back with a wave before following the trail downriver.

As he climbed in elevation along the Klappan River valley, the snowfall turned heavier, getting much deeper on the trail. At nights he found shelter beneath the larger pines where less snow accumulated.

The nights turned cold, much colder than Stephen ever remembered back in Virginia in early October. Dry wood to start fires came from matchstick size dead branches from the lower portions of the pine and fir trees. The larger dead branches were used to get the fire crackling, and with the hatchet he chopped down one or two of the smaller dead trees, dragging them onto the fire, moving the larger pieces forward as they burned down. Standing dead trees were much dryer, but more scarce than those lying on the ground, which needed to be hauled into camp before dark.

He wore extra socks, pants and shirt to stay warm in the bedroll with pine boughs beneath it to keep off the cold ground. Fires were built closer to the lean-to shelter than usual and banked to last longer into the night.

He dreaded getting up and starting the fire in the mornings. One day particular spurred him to action, as snow had stopped during the night, and the skies cleared. Unsure of how cold it had turned, the solid frozen water bag was a good indication. He'd placed his boots beneath the pack but it did little to keep the leather from turning stiff and icy cold. His toes turned numb inside the boots by the time the fire was hot enough to place the boots near it. He melted snow to make a hot cup of tea and ate two hard flat biscuits for breakfast while trying to thaw the water bag.

Later in the day, he took an additional astronomic observation on the sun and updated his map in the area he'd hobbled through on the crutch. Soon, he came to the edge of the burn where the wolves had attacked, double-checking his rifle and carrying it cautiously as if he expected the remaining wolves to have awaited his return. The snow, now up to his knees and wet, made walking difficult.

Stephen could see the trail only where taller willows and leaf laden alder trees did not bend to the ground from the weight of the snow. This too, made it difficult to walk, with having to step over bent branches, knock snow off, or lift the branches to walk under, all causing frequent rest stops. His pants and boots were soaked through and he sweated from exertion; he was soaked from the inside as well as the outside.

Sitting on his pack looking up valley toward the end of the burn, he wondered if it would be easier walking once he was back in the timber. He knew there would be fewer willows, but the snow kept getting deeper the higher he climbed.

He remembered, too, that once he reached the top and dropped back down along the Nass River, he would climb again even higher, further up the Nass before dropping again onto the Skeena. He shook his head at the thought. What should have taken three days would take at least twice as long, if he could keep up his strength.

He'd wished for snowshoes when he entered the burn and began struggling through deep snow. Now as he sat on the pack, his mind pictured a snowshoe and how it was constructed, though he hadn't seen one since leaving Virginia. Stephen looked at the scattered willows growing in the burn, wondering if he could weave or tie together a makeshift snowshoe. He rummaged through his supplies, retrieving everything he could use to lash willows together—rope, extra leather shoe laces, and fishing line. He spent most of the day trying different diameters of green willow; bending, notching, cutting, splitting short segments and working a separate branch into the splits; lashing pieces together and testing; finally constructing two workable snowshoes with toes that curved up in the front. Stephen cut one of his shirts into strips to lash the snowshoes to his jackboots.

Wet snow clung to the green willows, not only building up beneath the shoes, but between the snowshoe and his boot heels. Having to stop often to kick and scrape the snow free and lifting the shoes to step over branches was difficult, even without weight of the wet snow. But it wasn't nearly the effort as it would have been without them.

He walked past the place where he'd shot the two wolves without recognizing it. Rounding a small ridge, he could see the end of the burn and had started down the slope, picking his way through small trees and willows when a snowshoe tip caught on a willow branch, tripping him forward down the steep slope. He put his hands out to catch himself but they sank into the deep snow and the rifle slung over a corner of the pack flew forward, whacking him on the side of his head.

With his face buried in the snow and the heavy pack resting on his neck, he reached for solid ground with his hands, but couldn't touch it.

Struggling to upright himself, his head and shoulders worked deeper into the snow. Assessing his predicament, he began to laugh at himself. He was stuck solid. He tried lifting the snowshoes, but the snow held them firmly, and the humour of it hit him again. Finally, the seriousness of the situation sunk in, and his thoughts turned to that of dying right here, trapped face down in the deep snow.

He worked an arm up to the surface, feeling for willow branches and luckily found several close together to hold his weight on. With the aid of the rifle butt jammed in the snow, he pushed upward, and the slow-healing rib felt a jab of pain from the strain. He pushed harder and rolled to the side, allowing him to free a snowshoe. He wondered if the rib broke again and probed it with a finger, determining that he hadn't re-broken it. Struggling further, he sat upright, wiping snow from his face, and looked up at the sky and gave thanks. A short time later he walked out of the burn and into the timber where he made camp for the night.

The next four days proved very difficult, as most of the hiking was without benefit of a trail where less vegetation grew. Many of the poplar treetops bent considerably from the unusual amount of early wet snow. They'd not yet lost all their leaves and the smaller, thinner ones bowed to the ground, while many broke off halfway up their trunk.

Several stops were needed to repair the snowshoes; the round willow cross pieces worked free of the bindings, and dragged in the snow, or a piece broke and needed to be replaced. He'd anticipated breakage and brought along several short pieces of willow branches for such repairs.

At camp a few hours from the divide between the Nass and Skeena watersheds, Stephen found an ancient tree stump still firm and solid. He tried splitting firewood from the top and chopped at it several times, discovering the wood to be extremely hard. The pieces coming loose had a strong pine smell, full of hardened sap. He suspected the pitch filled wood would burn readily, so carved off thin slices, touching a lit match to the shavings. Pleasantly surprised, they burned like a candle with black smoke. Placing small dead branches on the flames soon produced a warm fire.

Deciding to take along small pieces of this pitchy wood, he placed his jack-knife blade at the end of a piece, attempting to split it as he pulled the blade toward the hand holding the wood. Suddenly the wood split and the knife blade came back against the top of his thumb. He flinched from the sharp pain, seeing he'd sliced the thumb open in front of the nail, from the tip to the depth of the thumbnail. The cut ran alongside the bone, and the lower part of the thumb hung down, creating a wide gap. It looked ugly and started to bleed. He quickly pocketed the knife and grabbed the thumb with his other hand, holding the gap together, thinking of what to do. How many times had his father told him to never cut toward himself with a knife? He should have known better, he thought. Danged dummy!

He knew if he didn't wrap the split thumb tightly and in its proper position, it would never heal correctly. Also, there was the possibility of losing it to infection, like Vega had lost his leg from the grizzly attack. He dug out the medicine tin once again, put iodine around the cut and used much of the remaining gauze to wrap it tightly. Surprisingly, there was not much blood from the wound, but he knew if he didn't protect it somehow, it would be very painful, as well as difficult to heal. Stephen thought of different methods to protect it, finally taking a tin of small fish packed in oil from the rations. Fish and dried biscuits would be his supper.

Stephen used his knife blade to slice along the top of the five-inch long rectangular tin, realizing how difficult things would be without use of his left thumb. He dumped the fish into a small pot and cleaned the lid of remaining fish oil, then sliced a thumb-wide strip off the lid and bent the strip into a U shape, placing it over the thumb, a half inch above the top. He then wrapped the remaining gauze around the tin shield, holding it firmly in place.

Lifting up his handy work, which made the thumb look over twice the normal size, he exclaimed in his best British accent, "It's 'rother a 'nosty lookin' thumb there old chap, but a 'smoshing' bit of work you've done. A gentleman such as yourself should patent this wonderful splint. Sell it to all the 'ospitals, you would," and laughed at the sorrowful-looking, large white thumb.

After reaching the divide that marked the drop down onto the Skeena River, Stephen finally found the trail. He'd walked along the divide in each direction before finally recognizing the place where he spent three days shivering in his bedroll. Curious, he dug to bare ground, finding the snow to be a full four feet deep. Without the willow snowshoes he would've never made it this far. Now, halfway to Kispiox Village, he'd used up more than half the food rations. He hoped the snow depth would lessen as he dropped down toward the river.

Before dark he came to the lake he'd passed in the rain on his way up, so he pitched camp for the night. The lake wasn't frozen but ice had formed along the edges. He saw a couple of ripples on the surface and knew there were fish in the lake. He quickly gathered firewood then rustled through his pack, finding the two fish hooks he'd stashed. He took apart a portion of a snowshoe that had been lashed together with fishing line. He'd bumped the bandaged thumb several times throughout the day, causing a throbbing pain, so tried to be extra careful working with his hands.

He kicked three feet of snow off several short dead logs, rolling over each one before finding a couple of earth worms. Working one onto the hook, he cautiously picked his way along a fallen tree jutting out into the lake. He stopped when he could no longer see bottom and squatted down for balance, holding onto a foot high dead branch. In less than a minute he felt the nibble, set the hook, and pulled out a twelve-inch trout with orange-coloured slits beneath its gills — a fine native cutthroat. A chunk of worm remained on the hook as he took the trout off and tossed the fish back into the deep snow. Before running out of worms, he had five trout, each slightly larger than the last. He fried two for supper, the meat being firm and pink, tasting even better than he remembered the fresh steelhead trout in California. He wrapped the three fish in the empty cloth flour bag and placed them in the snow to cool.

While lying beside the flickering fire on his bedroll beneath the lean-to shelter, Stephen pinpointed the last areas on his map that would need a sextant reading on the sun in order to show accurate details through the area where rain had been long and hard. He put the map away and lay back on the bedroll, placing his hands behind his head, reflecting on the past few days and the trail that lay ahead. A lone loon gave an eerie warble from the lake, and the smell of burning wood drifted into the shelter on a waft of smoke.

He thought about Ryan Evers, wondering where he had gone and if he'd survived. He'd probably stashed his backpack near where Jock was killed, so was not without food. As long as he didn't have a gun, Stephen felt safe. But yet he had a feeling in the pit of his stomach that bothered him, like a speck of dirt in an eye: you know it's in there somewhere, but can't quite figure out where.

Then he thought of Mariana, reliving their moments together and of how their fondness grew in such a short period. He also thought of her concern for his safety here in the north country and how lightly he'd put it off, having no foresight of how rugged this country would be; how things could happen in a moment's time that could mean life or death. He reflected back on the various incidents, hoping he'd seen the last of them, then remembered the second letter he'd written to Mariana. He still carried it in the pack and wondered if it would be too late when he returned. After all, he had told her to look for someone else more dependable than himself. He regretted having said it, thinking more of her than he had of Rachel the whole trip. Was it because he'd inadvertently given up hope of ever seeing Rachel or Michael again.? Did he truly have a right to go his own way now, pretend he was no longer married? Who could he turn to to help find the answers, he wondered. A priest? The law? Perhaps there's a written law that says, after so many days of not knowing if someone is alive or not, the marriage is no longer valid. It was all so confusing. Struggling with many different thoughts, he finally fell asleep.

CHAPTER 11

THE TELEGRAPH CONSTRUCTION CREW PRESSED FORWARD FROM Fort Fraser, heading westward to the Wa Dzun Kwua River and Hagwilget Canyon where the line crossed the river above the village. The line workers re-decked the narrow bridge that Stephen had crossed and they reinforced it with strips of rawhide. When it was completed, a hundred and five white workers, many Chinese cooks and Indian packers crossed over the bridge. This reinforcement allowed them to take their two hundred pack animals and a herd of beef cattle across, with great difficulty, but without losing a single animal over the side. The Hagwilget natives had never before seen a horse, but had heard of this terrible Man-o-War as it was called by the coastal Indians. All the villagers attended the monumental bridge crossing, voicing their approval whenever an animal acted up and again when it was finally brought under control and stepped to solid earth on the other side. Working along the Wa Dzun Kwua River, the crewmen renamed it Bulkley after the head of operations back in San Francisco, Colonel Charles F. Bulkley and the name Bulkley River would stick over the years and become a famous steelhead river for fly fishermen, as did the Kispiox River, retaining the largest wild steelhead in the world. From Hagwilget, the telegraph line ran northward to the Skeena River across from the Kispiox Village. Edward Conway arrived by boat to oversee line completion to Kispiox.

At twenty-two years of age, Charles Morison was instrumental in helping bring a fleet of 25 canoes loaded with construction supplies and food rations to Kispiox. Conway had sent Morison and another man to parlay with the Kispiox shaman, who'd convinced the people of the village that salmon would no longer come up the river if the telegraph wire stretched across it. Morison took tobacco as a bargaining tool, and after heated discussion among the villagers, they banished the shaman, allowed the telegraph line to be strung across the river and enjoyed the prized tobacco.

The men built a supply house at Kispiox, naming it Fort Stager, after General Anson Stager, the superintendent of military telegraphs whom Colonel Bulkley had served under and gained expertise on telegraph construction.

In early October, the telegraph wire hummed with messages from Fort Stager to New Westminister, and poles had been erected to where Stephen had begun his survey. After the early snow storm and cold weather slowed progress, Conway ordered operations to halt for the winter.

Following Morison's parlay with the Kispiox people, Morison and a company bookkeeper named R A Brown were assigned to return down the Skeena by canoe, then travel up the coast to the Stikine River. Here they were to hire natives and canoes to pick up supplies stored at the river's mouth and ferry the goods upriver to Buck's Bar. Explorer Pope's negative report of a possible route across country to the Stikine, along with the disappointing report of the two returning surveyors who had explored the Nass watershed, left all hopes for a spring startup hinging on Stephen Doyle's finding a route. Conway hoped beyond measure that Doyle would return with a favorable report.

On October 10, Stephen left the lake camp and started toward the Skeena River. The trail on the east slope of the mountains proved easier to follow, being in dense forest with a lesser snow depth. The occasional view through the trees of the high, rugged and nearly totally white snow-covered mountains to the east was a captivating scene, especially one late afternoon. The setting sun shot through an occasional break in the clouds to cast its final pinkish-orange rays of light on the snow-capped peaks. These opalescent colours, punctuated with intermittent dark patches of rock cliffs hanging on the mountainside, contrasted the dark evergreen trees marking out the timberline of the pine forest, a truly enchanting view. Stephen wished Hugh were here to see this rugged, mountainous country at its most colourful moment.

Stephen's belt had to be taken up a notch from losing weight due to strenuous activity and the small amount of food. His leg, back and shoulder muscles had tightened, becoming firm and hard. The wound from the wolf attack healed, but still caused pain on occasion. He felt strong enough, but his strength had been slowly diminishing, the poor diet taking its toll.

Two days later, Stephen took off the snowshoes and strapped them to his pack. The snow depth had decreased to a foot and he made better time walking in leather jackboots. He was able to take the final observation of the sun with the sextant, making the calculations before nightfall.

He updated the map, recording latitude and longitude in his journal, along with descriptions of the terrain, tree species and sizes.

Another day of hiking brought him near the place he'd encountered the Bukwas. He wondered if the creature had survived; if it was able to find food. But what foods did it eat? He imagined it trying to kill game to survive with a broken leg. Perhaps the giant ate mostly berries and plant roots, but from the strong stench it emitted, he suspected it also ate dead, rotting animals.

Suddenly a large, strange-looking white animal stepped through the trees onto the trail and stopped, and looked directly at Stephen, two hundred feet away. It was travelling uphill, away from the river. The animal's long hair appeared to be a very light cream colour, standing out in the pure white snow. Long tufts of hair that stopped a foot above its front ankles looked like leggings. The eyes were black and two ten-inch elongated cone shaped black horns curved up and back from the head. This unusual looking animal, which intermittently chewed its cud as a cow would, was called a mountain goat and dwelt atop high rugged peaks most of the year. The Kuldo dancers had used the horns and skin of a goat in one of their dances, but used a misshapen head carved from wood. They'd not done this magnificent animal justice.

The white goat had come down off the higher slopes because of the deep snow and was headed for the lower mountains to the west. Once its curiosity of Stephen was satisfied, the goat ran straight up the slope, then slowed to a fast walk. Stephen moved down the trail to where it had stopped and examined the tracks. They were the same hoofed tracks he'd seen on his way north, smaller than moose, but larger than deer, and now he knew what animal had made them. His curiosity was satisfied.

Before nightfall, he was on the trail leading to the top of a deep gorge, and could see the crystal clear creek running along the bottom. He recognized it as the creek where he'd found and buried the two miners. The camp where they had met their death was only a short way through the trees and he decided he would camp there again. The foot of snow covering the small opening made it look different, almost forbidding. Stephen felt uneasy, perhaps because of the shallow grave below the large tree roots nearby or the odd impression of being watched. Looking around the opening and into the trees, he couldn't see any tracks in the snow.

Unsure of what caused the unnerving feeling, he decided to cross the deep gorge and camp on the other side, a ways beyond the creek. He thought about Ryan Evers again and wondered if he'd somehow made his way this far north.

While preparing another trout supper, Stephen thought he heard occasional heavy footsteps in the snow. He listened carefully but heard nothing more and attributed the sounds to a snow-laden pine branch bending under the weight, the snow slipping to the ground with a pronounced thud. He had been hearing intermittent thumps all day long as the warmer day melted snow. Then, he heard three successive thumps back in the trees, hidden by the dark night. Again, he thought they sounded more like heavy footsteps than falling clumps of snow, so he reached for his rifle. Was it Ryan Evers? Perhaps a prowling grizzly waited to run at him, still needing food before denning up for winter? Or was it the Bukwas he had speculated killed the two prospectors? Perhaps the fire was keeping away any animals that might be out there. He built the fire higher, keeping an eye toward the direction of the last noise, hoping he'd brought in enough wood for a long night if the noises continued.

Hearing nothing more, he relaxed and ate supper, keeping the rifle at his side. He sat by the fire a few hours, ears attuned for any sounds in the dark, and before crawling beneath the shelter, he built the fire up once again. Putting on dry pants and socks and slipping nearly dry shoes back on, he went to bed fully clothed, falling asleep with the rifle alongside.

At 2:30 a.m., Stephen awoke to rustling noises in his pack, which leaned against a tree near the foot of the bed. He slowly lift his head and the dimly glowing fire cast just enough light to see the outline of the wild animal rummaging in his pack. It was covered with hair, and he caught a brief scent.

Stephen suddenly sat upright and shouted "Haaaaaa, get the hell out of here!" The startled coyote leaped sideways at the sudden noise and vanished into the low lying brush.

Before lying back, he glanced up through the trees and noticed the changing colours of light that slowly made their way across the sky. He'd never seen the Northern Lights before, so he crawled out of the bedroll and pulled on a jacket.

Stephen stood where he had the most open view of sky through the tall trees and watched the display shoot out its ever changing, dazzling colours. The lights were like a silky drapery, with rays of yellowish green appearing and disappearing every few seconds. Some slowly streaked across the sky while others shot out quickly, and the display reminded him of the kaleidoscope he'd played with as a child. It seemed the very heavens had come to life in a constantly changing scene, causing him to say, "Wow," more than once. He stood until the back of his neck ached from the tightening muscles, watching nature's mysterious light show unfold across the cloudless sky. He would certainly enter this marvelous display into his journal come morning, but wondered how he could adequately describe it.

Stephen struck camp at 8:30, sleeping longer than usual. He observed the tracks of the coyote that worked its way to his backpack and then ran into the bush when frightened off. He found the trail and started down the valley, knowing he would be in Kuldo Village by next afternoon.

Walking a short distance, he remembered he'd intended to walk through the trees back at camp, wanting to see if the thumping noises had left tracks, or just clumps of snow. The wind picked up, as he continued walking and occasional noises in the brush caused him to stop, look about and listen. Each time he stopped, he heard nothing. But when he walked on, he would soon hear sounds again. Was he just hearing things, or was something out there paralleling, tracking, stalking?

He became edgy and walked faster in the foot deep snow. Listening to the noise of his own footsteps, he compared them to the sounds he'd been hearing in the bush; they were similar, yet different. The rubbing noise of his heavy cotton pants, and the pack rubbing on his hips might be making the difference. He slowed his walk, listening carefully, and heard another noise back in the bush.

Stephen no longer thought it was Ryan Evers. If so, the cowardly murderer would have waited until Stephen passed by then shot him from behind as he'd done Jock. He became concerned it might be a stalking grizzly, hoping for a last meal before hibernating. He didn't want to be caught with the pack on his back, restricting accurate rifle movement, so he decided to turn the tables and stalk the bear.

Removing the pack, he leaned it against a five-foot diameter spruce tree, undoing the cover to retrieve the pistol. He shoved the pistol in his belt and checked the cartridges in the rifle, then backtracked his own footprints for five hundred feet before leaving the trail. He walked quietly through the brush and timber, listening for further sounds. Looking uphill through the trees, he spotted tracks in the snow that appeared to parallel the trail. Nearing the tracks and seeing they were several feet apart, he suspected that an animal had bounded through the snow.

The area contained less brush than where he'd just passed through, allowing him to see further. As he stepped near the tracks, he glanced in both directions, not wanting a surprise attack. He scanned through the trees, stopping abruptly when he saw another track two hundred feet uphill. Did the bear circle around and now watched from the timber? Or were there two of them travelling together? The breeze blowing downhill revealed no grizzly scent. He stepped forward, looking into one of the tracks, jolted by what he saw. This was no bear track. This was Bukwas!

The eighteen-inch footprint was plainly visible in the snow. The heel itself was a good half-foot wide, and as he looked at the next footprint, he realized why he'd thought an animal had bounded through the snow. He took a long step to duplicate its stride but fell short by over a foot. The footprints seemed much larger than he remembered the prints of the injured Bukwas. He stared in disbelief, whistling softly.

His heart pounded, thinking of this huge creature stalking him, wondering if food was its intent. Were they truly meat eaters? Then he remembered the human-like teeth. The Bukwas had no fangs to kill its prey, but as big as they were, they wouldn't need fangs. There would be little problem in killing an animal, or a man, with those powerful hands and arms. He took a deep breath as he looked to where the tracks disappeared in the timber, exhaling loudly as he turned his eyes toward the second tracks, wondering again if this Bukwas had a partner or if it had circled him. He didn't want to shoot one of these wild giants. He just wanted to get down the river to Kispiox, turn in his report and go back home.

Stephen decided to slip back downhill, grab his pack and get out of the area before anything happened. Quietly, he backtracked down to the trail and hurried toward his pack. He came around the bend of the trail and saw where his earlier tracks had stopped in the snow, but didn't see the pack.

Stopping, he remembered the large spruce tree he'd leaned the pack against, thinking he'd leaned it against the downhill side or perhaps he was mistaken and set the pack off to the side. Maybe I'm just being too danged spooked, he decided, starting forward again, placing his feet in the earlier tracks to quiet his steps.

Approaching the tree, he froze in mid-stride, when from behind the tree he heard the canvas-covered pack being torn, then a rustling, like something rummaging through the pack. He glanced uphill and saw the same large tracks leading to the tree. His heart raced, adrenaline surging through his chest. The giant was no more than twelve feet away! Then he heard a sniffing sound and the pack suddenly tipped from behind the tree and rolled onto the trail.

"Oh no!" Stephen thought. "This thing is going to move down to the trail any second and..." It happened as quickly as he had thought it.

The huge dark form made one step into the middle of the trail, holding the last cutthroat trout from Stephen's pack. He could see only the tip of the tail and head of the twelve-inch trout on each side of the clenched fist. The creature looked down at the pack, as Stephen took a long stride backwards, looking up at the nine-foot tall giant only six feet away. Not only larger than the Bukwas he had helped, this one was a much darker colour, almost black with silver tips on the hair, and a large scar on the side of its hairless face.

Stephen's footstep alerted the creature, which quickly looked up. The small black eyes met Stephen's, and there was a moment of uncertainty for both man and beast. Stephen didn't know if he should raise the rifle quickly and fire. He couldn't miss the large bulky body, but would the bullet stop the giant before it grabbed him and twisted him to pieces? Or should he turn and run, knowing that if the creature wanted him, he was a goner anyway? The Bukwas hesitated, taken by surprise, having allowed the familiar creature to get so near, and the giant beast was now deciding what to do.

The giant looked at the rifle Stephen held at his chest, and remembering what its function had been previously, screamed wildly: "*Aaaaaawheeeeeuuuu!*"

The deafening sound resonated in Stephen's ears. Before he could react, the creature jerked the rifle from his hands, nearly breaking the finger in the trigger guard and banging his wrapped thumb. The giant then did the same as it had done a year ago, by raising the rifle above Stephen's head, breaking the wood stock with a powerful wrenching. The large hands then applied force to the barrel, bending it considerably before dropping it to the ground.

Stephen couldn't move, frozen with fear as he watched this feat of strength. The stench from the beast this close was even more overpowering than the other creature had been. His thoughts returned to the broken barrel he'd found over a month ago: the man named Frank had his head torn off; the other poor fellow's head had been stuffed in the crotch of a tree. It all made sense now, and Stephen knew what was coming next.

The creature drew back to strike a backhand blow. Seeing it coming, Stephen ducked while turning to the side, raising his shoulder. The heavy blow caught him on the upper arm below the shoulder, slamming him through the snow into the hard ground on the uphill side of the trail, his opposite shoulder taking the brunt of the fall. A sharp pain shot across his chest from the two powerful blows. The beast screamed again, ready to reach down and grab the frail human when, a different, menacing scream filled the momentary silence.

The giant looked up the trail to the second Bukwas it had been travelling with when they'd curiously paralleled the human's path. The large dark creature watched the other briefly, then looked back at Stephen, bending slightly to grasp the top of his shoulder. The second creature screamed again at the larger Bukwas. *"Wheeeeeooooooo!"* and began a series of deep guttural grunts while walking swiftly toward them. The giant released the grip on Stephen's shoulder and stood upright, waiting for its companion. Stephen turned his head to look up the trail at the other creature. The colour of this giant's hair was reddish brown, and it walked toward them with a marked limp.

CHAPTER 12

THE BUKWAS HAD NARROWLY SAVED STEPHEN'S LIFE BY ITS DISRUPTIVE screams. This creature approached with anger, emitting continuous grunts, stopping five feet from the larger Bukwas.

They stood, arms hung to their sides, looking at one another. They towered over Stephen, who tried raising to one elbow but the pain in his chest and shoulder proved too great. He felt an ache from the area of the broken rib and the bandaged thumb throbbed. Looking up, wondering what would happen next, he knew his destiny would be decided in a few seconds.

The large creature opened its mouth wide, emitting a piercing shriek, which then lowered in volume, changing to a sort of cackling sound for several seconds, ending with two powerful huffs. The smaller creature responded with a type of whinny, followed by several sharp whistles and ending with deep throaty grunts.

"They're having a serious argument here," Stephen thought as he watched the display, his eyes moving back and forth while each creature took its turn uttering the strange noises. What were they thinking? Could their intelligence be advanced to the point of actual communication through screams and grunts? Or was it merely an angry exchange such as two dogs would do before they attacked one another? The different sounds from each suggested they were communicating, and as Stephen considered the possibility, he wondered what each animal might have conveyed.

Then the large creature emitted a sound much like a woman's scream, softening to a cry not unlike a baby's. When the cry ended, the creature looked down at Stephen, then leaned back, tilting its head upwards to make several wailing sounds which ended as it leaned forward again. One arm lifted to the waist then dropped suddenly to the side. There was a moment of silence before the smaller creature reacted, and Stephen's eyes were already on it, waiting for the response.

The small Bukwas reacted with a low volume wail and ended by looking down at its injured leg, then issued the same guttural sounds as before, ending with a whistling noise. The large giant turned and took a step uphill, hesitated, then faced the smaller Bukwas, glancing down at Stephen, then back up to its companion. The small Bukwas vocalized one more time in a seemingly consoling manner, Stephen thought, a sound like the mew of a kitten, similar to what he'd heard on their first encounter. After a brief fixed look, the larger giant picked the cutthroat trout off the ground and walked uphill.

Stephen could hardly believe what he'd just witnessed. This smelly, reddish-haired giant creature that shouldn't even exist just saved him from having his head torn off.

He hoped that would be the end of it when the smaller giant suddenly reached down and grabbed Stephen's arm, standing him upright. He winced from the chest pain and cried out, causing the giant to release the grip. Stephen bent over, gasping loudly, then stood upright with a pained expression. The creature made the same mewing sound that had seemed to console the larger giant. Even in a painful state, Stephen chuckled at the notion, then winced as the chest pain returned.

The hairy giant placed a hand atop Stephen's shoulder and pushed down gently, causing him to sit in the snow where he'd lain. Then the giant turned and walked back up the trail, limping from the injured leg. Stephen watched until it rounded the bend out of sight. The terrifying ordeal was over.

Stephen felt his pounding heart slow back to normal and sat in the snow several minutes before testing his physical capacity to move about. He checked both shoulders and arms by working them back and forth, feeling soreness in each, but most of the pain came from the chest. He wasn't sure if the pain was internal or just bruised muscles. It hurt to take a deep breath, causing him to stop short and exhale slowly. He stood and found he could walk okay, but didn't think he should try shouldering the pack. Looking around, he decided he would camp beneath the large spruce tree to give the aching shoulders time to recoup.

Stephen worked slowly at unpacking the essentials from the torn pack. He wouldn't need the lean-to shelter tonight with the clear weather. With great effort, he cut pine branches with the hatchet to place beneath the bedroll, then gathered firewood for the evening and morning fires. The snowshoes tied to the back of the pack lay alongside the big spruce, unbroken.

By the time he'd finished and sat down to relax, the shoulder pains had subsided some, but chest pains remained.

Late in the afternoon, he made a small fire to heat water for tea and a tin of small fish packed in oil. He'd intended to eat that last trout for supper and hoped the big giant choked on it, picturing the trout getting caught in its throat, leaving the creature writhing on the ground. Oh well, he thought, the big smelly beast did spare his life with a little unfriendly persuasion from the smaller one. He chuckled at the thought.

Starting to eat the heated fish and hardtack, he heard footsteps coming down the trail. His pistol lay on the bedroll and he reached for it while looking toward the sound. The Bukwas limped toward him, something dark hanging below a hand. The creature stopped before reaching the small fire in the middle of the trail and stared at the blaze, puzzled. The Bukwas looked at Stephen, then back to the fire. Perhaps this forest dweller had seen a lightning-caused fire before but never one this close and wondered what the flickering coloured lights with smoke rising steadily from it might be. Stephen could almost read the Bukwas's mind.

The giant looked again at Stephen, then reached out, dropping a rotting moose leg near his bedroll. The other hand held out a clump of sweet-grass, the roots containing small round seeds, like grains of rice. Stephen took the grass, but drew back from the rotting meat, the smell more overpowering than the Bukwas itself. He looked up at the giant, whose eyes were back on the fire. Then Stephen looked again at the rotting meat and clump of grass, guessing they were brought for him to eat. The creature squatted, eyes focused on the fire and reached slowly toward the flame.

"No, don't touch it!" Stephen shouted.

The Bukwas pulled back as if understanding the words, glanced over at Stephen, then back to the fire, reaching out quickly before Stephen could say anything. When the flames touched the large fingertips, it jerked back with a guttural growl and made a rapid swipe with the back of its hand, scattering the fire across the snow. The hissing sounds and additional smoke from the doused wood made the Bukwas pull backward. The fire was gone and that's what had bothered the giant. It turned toward Stephen and made a whistling sound. The humour of the moment made Stephen smile, as the two faced each other no more than four feet apart.

In exchange for the moose leg, Stephen took a small fish from the tin and reached toward the Bukwas. The giant stared at the offering and leaned in, sniffing, testing the unusual smell. The Bukwas took the small fish, popped the morsel in its mouth, swallowed, then reached for another. Stephen handed each fish to the Bukwas, one at a time, and when they were gone, it wanted the tin. Stephen held back, fearing the sharp edge would cut its fingers or lips if it went after the oil. But the giant took the tin from his hand and licked the inside, the tongue not as vulnerable as Stephen had thought.

Realizing there were no more of the tasty fish, the Bukwas reached for the rotting meat and slid it closer to Stephen. Stephen scrunched his face, smelling the odor even more. He looked into the creature's eyes and forced a smile, nodding his head in approval. Satisfied, the Bukwas stood and walked uphill. Stephen heard branches breaking behind him, then heard the creature return. The Bukwas placed the broken end of a branch on the ground and tipped it toward Stephen. He put his hand out to deflect the fall, and as it settled on his bedroll, he saw the forked branch. It had given Stephen a crutch.

The giant stared down at Stephen, perhaps wondering what more it could do for the frail little two-legged creature setting before him, then turned and walked back up the trail. The giant creature stopped at the bend to look back, raised a hand to its forehead, then quickly put it down again. Turning, the giant Bukwas limped out of sight.

"*I'll be danged,*" Stephen said. "That is one smart critter. I think that Indian was right. Bukwas is not an animal!" The giant had remembered both the crutch, and wave Stephen had given on their last meeting. No one would believe this. He looked back up the trail and said, "Good luck to you, friend."

Stephen stood and tromped down the snow along the trail for a short ways, and with his new crutch, pushed the rotting moose leg down the snow-covered trail and over the side. He rebuilt a warm fire and lay on his bedroll, going over the extraordinary encounter with the Bukwas, trying to decide if he should put it in the journal. He would never forget the near-human qualities of the Bukwas. Could one human, unable to communicate with another, have done any better? Also, he would never forget the fear when the larger angry Bukwas stood over him. He knew he was going to die. It was a feeling he hoped to never experience again.

The following morning he rearranged his pack, covering it with the torn canvas. His shoulders ached worse than last night and the chest pains were still quite evident. He retied the snowshoes to the back of the pack in case they were needed again. Stephen kicked around in the snow until he found the bent rifle barrel, deciding to carry it back home as a souvenir of his encounter with the two giants.

Stephen tied the bent barrel to the pack, and with the bandaged thumb, tender chest, and aching shoulder muscles, struggled to get it on his back. He walked down the trail with a slight limp and a smile on his face, thinking how fortunate he was to be alive.

Near the end of the second day, he entered the Kuldo Village. The dogs barked out their warnings and several children ran toward him, remembering him from his first visit. He looked the same, except for torn pants and a longer beard. The group of men who'd been hunting caribou were now back in the village and two of the men sat by a lodge, wondering who this stranger was that attracted the children.

Stephen walked to the lodge of Kwabellem, who'd stepped outside to see what had stirred the dogs. Seeing his friend, he welcomed him warmly.

"Hello, Stephen Doyle. I have been worried for you. You are late in your return."

"Yes, I was delayed...many reasons," he said smiling.

"I can see." Kwabellem said, looking at the large dirty white thumb. "You break it?"

"No, no. It's just a bad cut. It'll be fine."

"Why do you limp? Cut your leg a little too?"

Unaware he still limped, he looked down at his leg, then back to Kwabellem. "Oh that. A wolf bite. I'll tell you about it later. I need to get this pack off. Could you give me a hand?" Kwabellem lifted the pack from Stephen's shoulders and leaned it against the front of the lodge.

"Want to tell me about that?" Kwabellem asked, looking at the bent rifle barrel with a piece of broken stock tied to the pack.

On the way to the village, Stephen wondered what to tell Kwabellem about the rifle. Knowing natives were hesitant to talk about Bukwas and with their seeming fear of them, he thought someone in the village should know of its intelligence and possible kindness. He'd decided he would tell Kwabellem, and then he could decide if he wanted to tell anyone else in the village. So answering Kwabellem's question he said, "I will tell you about it tonight, when the lodge fire burns low and we sit alone."

Later, when Kwabellum's relatives slept and the fire burned dimly in the pit, Stephen told him about the two miners he'd found and buried. When he began to tell of his first encounter with Bukwas, Kwabellem stiffened but continued to listen. When he finished telling about the Bukwas hobbling into the bush on a crutch, the native looked at him with a doubtful smirk.

"Hey, Stephen," he said, poking a finger in his chest, smiling, "are you sure you didn't eat that mushroom *before* you saw the Bukwas?"

"I swear to God," Stephen answered quickly, raising his open hand. "That's just what happened. I even recorded it in my journal that night."

"Okay, okay," Kwabellem said smiling and raising his own palm in a like manner. "I believe what you say. It is hard to picture in my mind, a Bukwas walking with a stick for balance."

Then he paused and his voice lowered, becoming serious. "I have seen Bukwas too. Only once, but I know he is real. I saw him for just a moment …big…tall…hair all over him. I didn't smell anything bad like you did, but then I wasn't that close, maybe fifteen or twenty canoe lengths. He was big all right." Shaking his head, questioning even now as he told it. "My father has seen two different ones and grandfather said he has seen many. Maybe there were more of them years before. My people have many legends of Bukwas. Some say they took children when they played amongst the trees. Some say they stole fish from the net and caribou from the hanging pole. It is also said they tore the heads off the ancient ones who still walk at Dumsumlow Lake. Although no dead people have been found that Bukwas has taken, we think of him to be a devil." Kwabellem looked intently into Stephen's eyes. "You are the first to have a Bukwas so close to you and live to tell of it.

Stephen nodded in understanding, then Kwabellem asked, "Tell me the rest. How did your rifle get broken and bent like a hunting bow?"

Stephen told of the second encounter in which he did fear for his life and how the Bukwas he had helped returned the favor.

The story finished, Kwabellem shook his head in amazement and said, "You are one lucky white man. The great God of your book the missionary showed me must have his all seeing eyes upon you."

"You're right, Kwabellem. I have thought that several times on this trip and I *am* very thankful. It has been as if God accompanied me the whole trip. I just hope He continues it. I've still a ways to go."

The following morning, Stephen wrestled with the thought of spending the entire day at Kuldo. But he felt guilty regarding his progress to deliver the information to the construction crew at Kispiox Village, that it was slower than Conway had hoped for. By noon, Stephen had decided to continue on. The pain in his chest was subsiding, and he believed it was caused from stretched muscles, although deep breaths still made him stop short. He would just take it easy on the return to Kispiox.

He informed Kwabellem of his decision to leave and arranged his pack, handing his friend the two handmade snowshoes as a gift. Kwabellem smiled, nodding toward the side of the lodge where two pairs of quality snowshoes hung. He'd traded beaver, pine marten and otter pelts for them three years ago. Kwabellem's wife, Cunismore, brought Stephen smoked salmon, jerked caribou and fresh porcupine meat. When Kwabellem told him what the fresh meat was, Stephen chuckled to himself, and thanked Cunismore for her kindness.

Kwabellem walked him to the edge of the village, pointing out a shortcut to the Kuldo River crossing, the grandson tagging behind.

Stopping to say their good-byes, Kwabellem said seriously, "If you tell your people of Bukwas, they will come to find him...like they did the gold at Buck's Bar. I know your people. They will come. They will hunt them all to kill or capture Katamnkniest, the Man of the Mountain, and put them in cages. If you tell your people where the gold you carry was found, they will come for that too. You must think of these things, my friend."

Stephen looked somber from the words of caution, nodding in understanding, saying, "I have not recorded the second meeting with Bukwas in my journal." Then chuckled as he continued. "Shoot, no one's going to believe that crutch story anyway. They'll say I spent too much time alone in the woods."

Kwabellem laughed, and they exchanged warm hugs with strong pats on the back, knowing they would not see one another again. Stephen called the grandson, Kuhnelawp, the child who liked to throw rocks, to him, and slipped a jackknife into his hand. He asked Kwabellem to tell him, "This is a gift that your grandfather will teach you to use so you don't cut your finger." He winked at his native friend, then turned and walked down the trail.

When Stephen arrived at the Kuldo River, the greenish-coloured water was lower than when he'd crossed further downstream. He decided to cross the river before dark, so he could dry his boots and pants by the fire and not have to walk in wet clothes the following day.

The trail led to a small ridge of black shale rock protruding into the river, disappearing beneath the current and reappearing on the other side. Stephen looked upstream to see twenty-foot cliffs of shale rock where the water between the narrow cliff, ran deep. A slow moving pool of water formed above the shale ridge. Below it, the water ran swiftly for two hundred fifty feet, then widened and slowed before rounding the bend to where he'd crossed before. Looking across the river he could see a likely looking campsite and plenty of dry wood, so he decided he would cross here, where others had crossed.

Walking back into the trees, he found a limb for a staff to assist with the crossing and returned to the shale ridge. Two reddish-coloured salmon splashed in the water at the foot of the pool upstream, their tails nearly white. These were the last of the spawning silver salmon, called Coho, one of the favorites of the Indians, after the sockeyes.

Stephen stepped into the cold stream, letting the water flow over the top of his boots, wincing at the icy feeling as it worked its way down. He took slow short steps, holding the staff on the downstream side for balance, the water reaching to his knees. At the center of the stream, a four foot wide chute carried the faster water. He needed to step across the chute and place his foot in the right place where the shale ridge reappeared.

Stephen extended a foot forward, but the swift flowing water caught it and swept his leg downstream into the staff. He struggled for balance while his eyes searched for a solid place to put his foot. The bottom of the staff slipped off the shale ridge, carrying his foot with it. Stephen flapped his arms frantically to keep balanced, but it was too late. He splashed face first into the chute, the heavy pack slamming his chest against the water.

The cold shock along with the chest pain, caused him to exhale most of the air he'd sucked in before he hit the water. Swept into the rapids, he opened his eyes, seeing only frothy water. He struggled to get his head to the surface for air, but the pack rode on his neck, its weight holding him down. He reached for the bottom with his feet, but the water was too deep and swift. Feeling the overpowering need for air, he knew he had to get the pack off before it was too late. He started to panic, struggling to free the arms from the pack, but with water pushing him to the surface and the pack holding him down, he could do nothing. It felt like his lungs would burst: they needed air and his mind screamed to take a deep breath. He couldn't hold it a second longer. He had to let go, knowing this would be the last breath he would ever try to take.

He hadn't felt the top of the pack catch on the end of a four-inch dead hemlock tree, protruding six inches above the surface, it roots attached to the river bank. The swift current sucked the bottom of the pack beneath the water and Stephen's head popped to the surface, just as he gasped for air. The strong inhale took in life-saving oxygen, as well as water running down his face. He coughed violently, thinking the rapid's swift movements were creating air pockets. He couldn't think straight.

Another gasp for air was followed by coughs, and his eyes began to focus on the top of the trees downstream near the bend of the river. Then he saw the beautiful white clouds against the blue sky above the trees and his mind finally registered the scene, along with the water that flowed swiftly past his head, curling around the top of the pack and splashing his face. His legs floated downstream as he lay on his back, suspended by the tree. He was unsure of what had happened, what had brought his face to the surface and saved his life. He half expected the reddish-brown Bukwas to pull him out of the water any second.

Stephen reached his right arm up and behind, feeling the four-inch tree, then worked his hand to the top of the pack where it had caught on the rope wrapped around the canvas cover. He realized what had happened, what allowed him to see blue sky and clouds and trees again, and he couldn't believe it. He'd faced certain death once more and was spared, at least for now. Stephen knew he had to get out of the extremely cold water as soon as possible.

Gripping the tree, he pulled himself upstream enough to work his other arm out of the shoulder strap. The current pushed his shoulder sideways enough to grab the dead tree with the free hand; then he worked the other shoulder from beneath the strap and slipped the arm out. Floating on the stream surface while hanging on the end of the tree, he wondered how to retrieve the pack from the tree's grip.

Water had been working its way inside the pack, and as it filled, the swift water pushing against it proved to be too much weight for the tree end. Suddenly, the end of the tree broke. He floated downstream with the pack alongside and he grabbed a shoulder strap, then pulled the water-soaked pack closer as its weight carried it toward the bottom. Kicking his legs, he swam toward shore with one arm, but the strong flow carried him downstream around the corner.

The current swept him close to the bank as it rounded the corner and he reached his feet for the bottom, but couldn't touch it. He remembered the crossing he had used before, a quarter mile downstream.

Stephen's body began to feel numb and his actions slowed, he gripped the pack with a fist that didn't want to stay closed. He had to save energy until he got near the old crossing, paddling or kicking only enough to keep afloat. He stayed as near the southern bank as possible. If he didn't get out at this crossing, he would be swept into the large Skeena River.

Two hundred feet before the riffles flowed over the crossing, he touched bottom, struggling to keep the pack close, the heavy weight difficult to drag from the current. He worked closer to the bank, half walking, half floating, and was soon able to stand in the waist-deep water, pulling on the pack. The cold water had taken its toll, and he could barely move. The chest pains returned, causing groans each time he pulled the heavy weight. Finally, the pack touched bottom and he was barely able to slide it onto the boulder-strewn bank.

Stephen lay on his back on the rocks, shivering from the freezing cold October water. When his chest finally stopped heaving and he caught his breath, he struggled to rise, then staggered through the willows into the timber, finding a camp spot for the night. He gathered wood quickly in his heavy, sopping wet clothes, shivering uncontrollably, then returned to his pack, dragging out the wet clothes and tarp shelter. He worried about his map wrapped in oilskin, hoping it had kept dry. The waterproof match tin had done its job, and he was extremely grateful to whoever had invented it.

Stephen huddled over the small twigs piled on the bare ground where he'd kicked away the snow. With hands shaking severely, holding them on the ground to keep the match flame steady, he was elated to see the small flames lick their way through the small pieces of wood. The twigs crackled from the heat and he cupped his hands around the flames, then placed larger pieces on top as the fire took hold.

Shivering by the roaring fire, Stephen slowly dried his belongings. He wrapped the wrung-out damp inner wool blanket of his bedroll around his naked body, turning often to keep momentary warmth in.

Stephen thought about this latest experience, reliving it over and over, and was very grateful for the dead tree that had fallen in the river, miraculously pulling his head above water. A few inches more to the side and the pack would have missed the tree completely. Once again, he thought he was going to die, and he took time to thank God for the miracle, but inwardly wondered what else could go wrong on this trip that he'd thought would be so easy.

Fortunately only a small amount of water worked its way into one edge of his map. The journal had also been wrapped in oilskin and the extra folds kept it completely dry. He untied the wet gauze from his thumb and eyed his handiwork. The slice had healed together but had a noticeable red line where the two sides didn't meet evenly. He would still have to treat it with care for several more days.

Stephen finally fell asleep at 1:00 a.m., leaning against a spruce tree in a crouched position with the now dry blanket wrapped tightly around. But with the cold night and uncomfortable position, sleep came only in brief periods. The fire still glowed with coals when he decided he had enough of the forced attempt at sleep. Standing, he immediately noticed the burning sensation between his buttocks, then remembered he'd torn a couple of large leaves off the top of that devil's walking stick plant, to wipe himself last night. "That damned weed must've had teeny barbs on those leaves," he thought. "No wonder they call it the devil's stick. Damn thing is no good for anything." He never hated a plant as much as this one.

CHAPTER 13

CONTINUING HIS TREK HOMEWARD, STEPHEN KNEW HE WOULD soon come to the large pine tree where he'd started the survey. He'd thought about the large 'T' carved in the tree by the previous explorer, and to see it again had been his goal since leaving it over two months ago. When he finally did find the tree, there were newly constructed telegraph poles nearby. He looked down the line toward Kispiox Village and saw a twenty foot wide cut-line. Stephen followed the cut line to the edge of the village and on past it to the Skeena River where he spotted a rough log building with the name, *Fort Stager* painted on a sign above the door. A telegraph wire came off a nearby pole and attached to the side of the building. He leaned his pack against the structure.

As he swung the door open, he noticed the building was filled with wood boxes containing rations, large coils of wire and wooden barrels of insulators and brackets for line construction. In the small room to the side of the door, a slim man, forty years of age with thinning hair and slightly grey sideburns sat, holding a book on a small rough wooden desk. On the desk sat the telegraph key to send messages with and a sounder to receive. When sending, the lever would be depressed causing a circuit break picked up by the sounder at the other end of the line.

"Well, hello there, mister," the man said as he stood and faced Stephen. "You wouldn't be Doyle, would you?"

"Yes, I am. You must be the foreman of the pole line. Where's the rest of the crew? I didn't see them up north at the end of the poles."

"Well, no, I'm not the foreman of the line. I'm the telegrapher. The crew pulled out two weeks ago when the snow storm hit and it turned twenty below three days in a row. The foreman sent a message to Conway, and he said to pack it in for the winter. Conway was here when the crew strung line across the river. He returned to New Westminster right after this storehouse was started."

When Stephen first saw the end of the constructed line, he believed his delay was the reason it went no further, and the crew would be waiting for his report. He'd pushed himself for nothing. The time he'd lost for various reasons would not have made any difference. If all had gone smoothly, he might have made it back to Kispiox just as the snowstorm hit. He felt disappointed in the way things had worked out, as he had hoped for different results.

"Why are you still here?" Stephen asked.

"I've been waiting for you. My orders were to wait here until you returned and then contact Conway as soon as you showed up. By the way, my name is Stanley Mitchell. Is your partner outside?"

"Oh...ah, glad to know you, Stan." Stephen said, extending his hand in greeting, ashamed to have to be reminded of Jock.

"My partner, Jock Dubois...met with a serious accident. He's dead. I had to bury him." Stephen stared at the floor.

"Sorry to hear of it," Stan said quietly, also looking at the floor as a token of respect. Stephen changed the subject. "So what do we do with my maps and journal? The foreman was supposed to look them over when I returned."

"I'll send a message to Conway right now, let him know you're here. He'll tell us what to do. I suspect we'll both be headed downriver. I've got a twenty-foot canoe the company traded for and it's ready to go, but we won't know until tomorrow. Make yourself comfortable. I'll let Conway know that we'll be minus a man when we return. Jock Dubois, you said?"

Mitchell tapped out the message on the telegraph key while Stephen watched. When he finished, Stephen asked questions about the telegraph line—how the tapping signals worked, what different clicking noises meant, what the tapping was actually saying, how long would it take for the message to be received at the other end, how many telegraph offices there were, and more. Stephen had sent a telegram to his sister in Seattle, but merely wrote out the short message, leaving before the actual transmission. With an understanding of the system, his curious mind was satisfied.

The two spent the evening talking about the telegraph crew's work and their progress. Mitchell informed Stephen about the Atlantic Cable having been successfully completed in late July. It had been completed previously, but operated only 17 days before problems developed and the system failed. Because of the previous failure, the Western Union Extension Company decided to continue construction of their overland telegraph.

Unlike the undersea cable, whenever the overland telegraph failed for any reason, it could readily be repaired[12].

They also talked about Stephen's trip north. He didn't mention the incidents with the Bukwas, considering what Kwabellem had said to him in departing. Not that he would never tell anyone about the Bukwas, but he'd decided he most definitely wouldn't tell everyone about them.

Stephen had thought of the Bukwas encounters often during the previous few days and had vivid memories of both incidents, the second being the more frightening. He would never forget either. He'd also wondered how many people had actually seen a Bukwas, suspecting quite a number had, because of the people he'd come in contact with—the toothless old man at the Hagwilget bridge, the Kispiox native who stood by the long house, the Long Grass people, and finally Kwabellem. All were aware of Bukwas in some way. The Kispiox man said he wasn't afraid of them, but how would he know unless he'd seen one? Kwabellem saw one, his father had seen two and his grandfather, he'd said, had seen many. Jock saw tracks and heard a scream from one, his Indian guide telling him it was Bukwas. Then there was the scream on the coast when they gathered wood. Jock told him it was what he'd heard before. Also, there was the fishing guide in California who'd taken him and Hugh for steelhead trout. The guide himself never saw one, but heard stories of people in California who had. And finally he thought of his nightmare in San Francisco when he envisioned a giant hairy beast, much like the real thing, a premonition of what he would encounter on this exploration.

From this, Stephen speculated there may be more than just a scattered few of these strange giant hairy creatures. But why hadn't someone captured one, or killed one, or even found the bones of one that had died? He pondered these unanswered questions, supposing their isolation to be the main reason. Perhaps some day, someone else would find the answers.

"Oh, by the way," Stanley said when the thought came to mind, "A friend of yours is staying in the village. Asked me to keep it a secret. Said he wanted to surprise you, so I was supposed to get word to him when you came in. Just didn't trust him though. Something about him seemed a little strange. Thought I better let you know."

Stephen's puzzled look caused Stanley to continue. "He didn't leave his name but he's a big man. Do you know who he is?"

"Can you tell me anything else about him, like what he wore maybe?"

"Oh, just plain old cotton pants and flannel shirt. His hat was a dark brown felt with a narrow brim. Had a handlebar moustache."

"Yeah," Stephen said, "I know him," remembering the felt hat and moustache that Ryan Evers wore. He must have returned to where he'd escaped and retrieved his hat. Stephen also wondered if Evers found either his own rifle amongst the trees where he'd tossed it or Jock's rifle hidden beneath the leaves. His thoughts raced, knowing Evers waited here to kill him, like he had Jock. If he didn't have one of the two rifles, he'd probably bought one from a villager.

"Did he carry a rifle when you saw him?" Stephen asked.

"No, he didn't have one any of the times he was here. He's come by nearly every day now since the crew left, seeing if you showed up yet."

Stephen decided he'd better fill Stanley in on Ryan Evers and after doing so, asked Stanley if he owned a rifle.

"Oh, heavens no. I don't need a gun. I've only shot one a couple of times when I was a child. I don't hunt or anything like that, so never needed one. But the company left a rifle here. It's in the supply room." Stanley led Stephen into the room and showed him the old flintlock. It was nearly identical to the one Stephen had hunted squirrels with back in Virginia.

"Stan, you better take this pistol." Stephen said as he pulled Evers pistol from his belt and handed it to him. "Evers shot my partner in the back of the head, and he wouldn't hesitate to shoot you either if he has to. He's a killer, Stan, and if you have to use this pistol to save your life, then you dang well better do it."

"Oh my!" Stanley said as he hesitantly took the pistol. "I'm not sure about this. I don't know if I could kill someone." He turned the pistol in his hand, looking it over carefully.

"Stanley, Evers is going to come back here any time looking for me. If he has a gun and knows I've returned, he'll shoot you on the spot. So don't get all squeamish about defending yourself. I'm sorry you're a part of this now, but until we get an answer back from Conway, we don't have a choice. We have to be prepared for him. Here, I'll show you how to use it."

Darkness came at 7:00 p.m., and Stephen hung a blanket over the single window to keep Evers from seeing in. Stephen made out his bedroll near the door of the supply building and kept the loaded flintlock alongside.

It was almost noon the following day before the message from Conway came over the telegraph wires. Mitchell stayed close to the storage building, listening for the first taps to come across the sounder. Stephen took his rifle and wandered down to the confluence of the Skeena and Kispiox rivers where several of the village women fished with hand lines. He watched only long enough to see they were catching trout. He wondered what would happen if a 20 or 30 pound salmon like he'd seen spawning on the Kuldo River got hooked on one of their hand lines. He even visioned one of the large fish pulling a native woman right in the water, and her shouting out when her head bobbed above the surface, "I've got a big one on. Start the fire and I'll be back soon as I get him tired out."

Some of the women sat on the sand while others stood. There were five in all and they talked freely until one of them saw Stephen approach. All turned to see the stranger, then went back to their fishing, but with less conversation. One would turn to look at him, say something to the others, then another would turn, look away and say something else, all trying to stifle their girlish giggles. Stephen felt uncomfortable as he watched, imagining they were making fun of the white man, as he'd also imagined with the three young girls on the river bank and the two men carrying salmon to the village. He walked away quietly, wishing he could understand what they said. He didn't notice one of the women hurrying toward the village as he turned away.

He arrived back at the storage building just as Mitchell came out with the message from Conway. Their instructions were to return immediately to New Westminster, making haste to Fort Simpson on the coast where the company steamer, *George S. Wright*, would stop in eight days on its way south. They could get passage on the ship from there, and Stephen was to bring his information directly to Conway's office. Eight days would give them no time to wait around. They needed to hurry just to get there before the ship departed.

The two men locked the storage building and carried their packs to the canoe, looking over their shoulder constantly, in case Evers showed up. Stephen sat in the back, being the more experienced canoeist of the two, having crossed the Skeena River once before.

Stan Mitchell had been with the Western Union Extension Company for two years. His job was to man the station nearest the end of the constructed telegraph line in order to receive and send all messages concerning progress, construction material needs, supplies and even personal messages. He'd come from Montreal after he had heard about the need for qualified operators. The first trip into remote country had been an earlier posting to the small town of Yale on the Fraser River.

Of English descent and forty-four years of age, Mitchell stood at six-foot, had graying sideburns and wire rim spectacles. To Stephen, Mitchell looked frail, causing concern about his stamina to paddle a canoe all day long. But by the time they reached the Gitxsan Village of Gitanmaax, ten miles downriver, Stephen had changed his mind regarding Mitchell's energy. His thin arms and bony fingers proved worthy of the task, and Stephen had to work hard to keep up.

If they merely floated with the current, they would not make it in time to catch the ship. Continual paddling was necessary, and when one rested or switched sides, the other accommodated. Mitchell made the calls regarding the routes to take to avoid boulders and whirlpools, and if approaching rapids looked unsafe, they beached the canoe before entering the swift current, using a rope to handline through. They tied their packs and rifle to the canoe, in the event of a capsize, and the two men gradually learned various canoeing techniques.

Rounding a sweeping bend were the canoe bobbed along in two foot waves, a loud crack shattered the turbulent sound of flowing waters, and wood splinters from the top of the canoe sprayed both men. They turned quickly to see a canoe carrying three men bearing down, no more than 70 yards away. Two men from the village paddled, and in the middle sat Evers wearing his buckskin jacket and felt hat. The rifle he frantically reloaded was a single shot breech loading .50 caliber, owned by one of the Indians.

Unfamiliar with the rifle, Evers fumbled with the process, hurrying to get off a second shot before his quarry returned fire. The muscles around Evers shattered collar bone had healed but he had limited use of his arm, and pain from the wound still reared its ugly head.

Evers had been waiting around Kispiox Village for over a month. He had made his way to Gitanmaax Village six days after Stephen purchased supplies at the trading post. Evers found some medical assistance in the village after finding the trading post and questioning the bearded, tobacco chewing proprietor about a doctor. "Doctor," the proprietor had said. "Hell no. There ain't no doctor within two hundred miles. The Village has a shaman though. He'll fix you up pretty good. What's the matter with you?" After being told he was bush-wacked by a surveyor exploring for the telegraph line and showed the burly man his wound, the proprietor told him that he didn't think all the Indians' magic up and down the Skeena could fix that.

Ryan Evers stayed in Gitanmaxx Village for over a month, the shaman doing what he could to help heal the wound, before Evers travelled up-river to Kispiox and waited for Stephen Doyle's return. Evers had hung around the crew cutting trees on the telegraph line above the village, often times going ahead of them. He always carried a rifle and told them he was hunting moose. He'd been staying at the lodge of the pot-bellied man sitting in the front of the canoe, whose wife had been handline fishing that morning. Evers had told the natives he was a Colony constable, and one of these men was wanted for murder down at Fort Langley. The man named Doyle had shot him in the shoulder when he tried to arrest him. The other man, he'd said when he discovered the two telegraph company employees had left the village, was just as guilty for helping him escape. Evers had paid the Indian paddlers well to help him catch up to the two white men in the canoe ahead.

Stephen looked at the flintlock tied to his pack and knew he wouldn't be able to get it loose fast enough, without exposing himself to the next shot.

"Stanley," he said quietly, almost whispering. "Hand me that pistol fast, or we're both dead." Stan raised up on his knees and pulled the pistol from his belt, then handed it toward Stephen.

"Get down low Stan. He's about ready to shoot again." Stephen lay low in the canoe, his eyes peering over the top.

"*Faster!*" Evers shouted out. "Get me next to them before they get their guns out." The two men dipped their paddles deeper and pulled hard, but their strength was nearly gone from the strenuous effort already given. Evers rose to his feet and pointed the old rifle, looking for more of a target than the top of Stephen's head, which disappeared as soon as the gun came up. A wave tipped the pursuing canoe and Evers struggled to keep balanced, nearly falling over the side before setting back down.

"Pull harder you yahoos," Evers shouted. "We almost got them," then raised the rifle again. Stephen peeked over the back of the canoe and Evers fired.

"Ow!" Stanley shouted out and turned onto his back holding his shoulder. He pulled away his hand and looked at the slice through his shirt and the trickle of blood coming from the grazing wound. Stephen turned his head to see how badly Stan had been hit.

"I'm okay! Just nicked my shoulder," Stanley said. "Don't let him get off another shot. We might not be as lucky next time."

Stephen glanced at the flintlock and wondered again if he had time to get it free. He peeked back over the end of the canoe and saw Evers struggling to close the breech on his rifle, then begin to stand for another shot.

Stephen raised the pistol over the end of the canoe and cocked the hammer. He aimed for Evers chest, now 25 yards away, and pulled the trigger. The bullet caught Evers just below his armpit, spinning him sideways. His dropped rifle struck the edge of the canoe, then bounced over the side, swallowed up by the fast moving water. Evers staggered and reached for the rail of the canoe, but the wet wood caused his hand to slip off into the water, and the shattered collar bone showed no mercy when he grabbed for the rail as he went over the side.

The canoe nearly tipped over and both Indians grabbed hold to keep from going in. When the canoe uprighted, the Indian in front reached down and snatched up another rifle, then took aim.

Stephen recognized the man as the one with the pot belly and low riding pants he'd spoke to in the village on his way north. Stephen ducked and the bullet slammed into the side of the thick wood dugout, just below the top.

Stephen rose to his knees and pointed the pistol. "Don't make me kill you," he shouted. "I've got five shots left and I'll put all of them in you before you reload."

The potbellied man looked up from his rifle and saw the pistol pointed directly at him. He slowly raised the rifle in surrender. "Throw it over the side!" Stephen ordered.

The man looked at his rifle, hating to part with it. It had cost him four full-size grizzly hides, tanned and softened by his wife.

"Throw it in the river or I'll shoot," Stephen said. The Indian looked at the rifle again and knew the money in his pocket from Evers would buy him a new one. He let it drop into the river.

"*Help! I'm gonna' drown,*" came a voice from behind the natives' canoe. "I can't keep afloat. Get me out of here."

The Indian at the rear turned to see Evers' head bobbing in the water. He reached his paddle toward him.

"*Drop the paddle!*" Stephen said forcefully. The Indian turned and saw the pistol pointed at him this time and pulled the paddle into the canoe, laying it gently on the floor, keeping his eyes on Stephen.

"Get me out of here you damn rotten Indians, and hurry it up, or you won't get the rest of that money. "

"*Nobody's getting you out, Evers,*" Stephen shouted back. "*Your killer money is going to end up in the bottom of the river, just like my partner Jock. He's probably waiting for you downstream. He'll be real glad to see you.*"

"*You sons-a-bitches,*" Evers shouted back, then disappeared beneath the surface. His head popped up briefly and a strange gurgling sound was heard, followed by a violent stirring for several seconds, then it became still. The four men gazed at the water, looking for some additional sign from the drowning man, each reflecting on their own thoughts of that particular way to die, none liking the idea.

"You men head for shore," Stephen said. " Your job's done. Go on back home."

The two natives looked at one another, the one in front nodding his head and speaking to the other man. They paddled toward shore, wondering how they would get their dugout back to the village.

Stephen gave an audible sigh of relief. Stanley smiled and nodded in agreement, then looked at his shoulder wound.

"How is it, Stan?"

"It'll be okay. Lets find a camp spot though. I've had enough for today."

The two travellers were themselves weary from the afternoon's work, and while watching for a campsite, they suddenly realized they were being propelled toward a chute of rapids. The frantic paddling for shore became fruitless as the canoe pitched over the waves, crashing into the next swell.

They struggled to keep the front end pointed directly downriver, with waves tossing it as it would a small log floating freely along. Twice, they found themselves holding onto the rails, hoping for the best. The second time it happened, Mitchell dropped his paddle, nearly capsizing the canoe when he lunged after it. The paddle drifted out of reach. Stephen took over from the rear, switching his paddle from side to side, dragging it in the water to keep the heavy canoe pointed downriver. They were relieved to see calmer water just before rounding the bend, but the loose paddle was no longer in sight. Once in safer water, Stephen shouted, "*Wooo weee!* That was some ride, Stanley. Let's go back upriver and try it again. That almost beats sleigh riding back in Virginia."

Stanley looked over his shoulder with an ashen face and said, "No thanks, just find a place to pull over. This has been a much too invigorating day for me."

They spotted a sandy beach with large overhanging cottonwoods lining the bank, and Stephen landed the canoe at the tail end of the sand. The canoe had several inches of water in the bottom and Mitchell's entire front dripped with water that had splashed over the bow.

After the fire took hold from the damp, smoky cottonwood tree limbs, and their camp was set up, Stephen dressed Mitchell's shoulder wound, which was more like a deep scratch and would heal in a short time. Stephen searched for a six-inch wide dry piece of wood from which he could chop, carve, and whittle out another paddle. He worked on the paddle until late evening, taking time to eat the meal Mitchell prepared—boiled caribou jerky, beans and hardtack, with hot tea.

They went over the day's events and, Stanley asked Stephen if he had ever killed anyone before this.

"No, I never have." Stephen said. "I guess you don't really know what you'll do until your back is against the wall. You don't have much time to think about it. You just know it's either you or him. Same thing happened with Evers that first time…after he'd killed Jock. When he came around that tree, I knew if I didn't shoot first, I was a goner." Stephen stared down at the ground, his voice turning softer. "You know Stan…Jock was the first man I've ever seen killed. One minute he's there…happy to be alive, enjoying what he liked to do best. Next minute, he's gone…forever… never to laugh again at his own jokes. It hit me pretty hard."

Stephen looked up at Stanley. "It's something I'll never forget." After a few moments of silent reflection, the two turned to other subjects.

The next few days went smoothly for the novice canoeists. Stephen occasionally entertained with songs, each in a different accent. Some, a bit raunchy, causing Stan to laugh. Many of the songs had been picked up in the various survey camps, when extra axemen and chainmen who'd come from different countries were hired on as additional helpers.

Floating along quietly, they saw several black bears and moose along the river bank, and one lone grizzly. One cool afternoon, they saw three flocks of greater sand-hill cranes heading south for the winter. The first flock had over eight hundred birds and the sky was nearly covered with their uneven flight pattern. The second flock was even larger, over a thousand. Their constant gurgle-like calls could be heard far off in the distance. Stephen remarked that it must not have turned so cold north of Buck's Bar; otherwise the cranes would have flown south earlier. The men also frightened many ducks off the water, particularly the fast flying mergansers which always flew close to the water, either up or downstream, depending on the proximity of the canoe.

Arriving at tidewater some forty miles from the coast, the men worked even harder to paddle the heavy canoe, the current from the river no longer helping. Occasionally, though, they were moved along by an unseen current that mystified them both. Here they saw a number of lone seals, their heads appearing above the water like small logs floating vertically, curious about the canoeists.

Stephen and Stan came to the mouth of the Skeena River in the early afternoon. With the aid of a map Conway had left at Fort Stager, they picked their way northward past the many islands to Fort Rupert.

CHAPTER 14

ENTERING THE BAY AT FORT RUPERT, STEPHEN AND STANLEY PADDLED their canoe past a schooner and small paddle-wheel steamer at anchor. They had a good view of the well-protected Hudson's Bay Trading Post. It was the second post established by the enterprising trading company along the Pacific coast. The first fort was built at the mouth of the Nass River by Captain Aemilius Simpson, Superintendent of the Marine Department of the Hudson's Bay Company. However this initial site proved unsatisfactory because of the difficult approach from the sea, due to severe winds and the occasional frozen sea water during colder winters. In 1834, the Fort was dismantled and moved to the current location, renamed Port Simpson in 1880, fourteen years after Stephen and Stanley first gazed upon it.

Two walls protected the trading fort, each constructed with two-foot diameter trees. The outer wall had pointed pickets ten to twelve feet high, and the main wall inside was nearly twenty feet. Only the tops of the two-storey buildings inside the fort could be seen from the bay. The four corners of the main wall had tall towers containing cannons, and the massive main gate was made of two strong doors studded with large iron nails to prevent attackers chopping into it.

Off to the side of the fort was an island housing a large number of Indians, and just beyond the garden area surrounding the fort, additional large native longhouses were scattered about in the trees and strung along the shoreline in both directions. Stephen estimated over a thousand people lived around the fort.

They landed their canoe alongside others tethered with lengthy ropes, because of the twenty-foot tides. They pulled their gear out and walked toward the large closed gates. They saw a small door swing open, allowing two men to exit. Several natives, men and women, were walking toward the entrance. Most carried trade items: baskets of dried salmon and halibut, fresh clams and lobsters, eulachon oil, and a bundle of wood.

Three women arrived at the gate ahead of the two weary travelers. Each glanced several times at the newcomers carrying large packs on their backs, and Stephen and Stanley heard the women whispering as they walked. One of the women pulled the door open, holding it for the other two, then looking at the two approaching men, stepped inside and closed the door. The two men looked at each other as the door was shut, wondering if they should just walk in as the women had done, or if they should shout out and wait. Stephen shrugged his shoulders and reached for the wooden handle, pulling the door open. As he looked in, he could see a number of people in the large open courtyard. No one looked toward the gate, so he stepped inside with Stan directly behind.

The courtyard was ringed by two-storey buildings painted white, the paint made from local clamshells. Warehouses were to the right and left, officer quarters and mess hall directly ahead, the trade store to the left. At the store entrance they pulled off their packs and Stanley went inside to inquire about the company ship, the *George S. Wright*. When he returned, he told Stephen the ship had not yet arrived, and they would need to talk to the commanding officer about staying the night inside the fort.

While Stanley went to the officer's quarters, Stephen sat next to the trade store, watching people in the courtyard. Listening closely, he could hear English, French, Russian and native Indian languages spoken. He marveled at the amount of trading taking place within the small area.

Between the doors to the various buildings, small booths had been built to accommodate various traders. One booth had guns and ammunition, another blankets and cloth. There was a booth with molasses, salt, sugar and spices, and one with tobacco, cigars and pipes.

The Hudson's Bay Company encouraged trade inside the fort, knowing that much of it would return through their own store. The Company not only traded for hides and furs, but for food items as well. Their inventory for goods just from the Indians for the past week included, 11 beaver skins, 20 deer, 187 dried salmon, 192 lbs of eulochon grease, 16 gallons of whale oil, ten pieces of goat meat and two of beaver meat.

At times there were large numbers of people around the fort, particularly during May and June when the Tsimshian people returned from the eulachon fishing grounds on the Nass River. One year during a twelve day period, 850 canoes with an average of ten people per canoe paddled into the small bay. Nearly 10,000 people camped or lived around the fort during this trading time.

Stanley returned shortly and had been told the large gates were opened only when quantities of trade goods were hauled in and out, but at dark the small entrance gate was locked, and the only people allowed inside at night were the thirteen company employees. The two would have to pitch their camp outside the fort, away from the gardens. They were not to pick any of the vegetables, which included radishes, cucumbers, cabbages, carrots and potatoes. The commanding officer suggested the two men camp in back of the fort, closer to firewood.

Walking through the small gate door and around the outside wall, they noticed a large number of graves. In 1862, the worst disaster to ever hit the Colony of British Columbia devastated the native people. A small pox epidemic, which the Tsimshian elders thought to be a product of some spiritual power, ravished the unsuspecting population. Over 500 had died at Fort Rupert alone, many of them children.

Stephen and Stanley found the charred remains of a campfire surrounded by rocks. The ground appeared a bit uneven for bedrolls, but they decided it would do for the night. It took over an hour to find enough wood for their evening and morning cooking fire, as everything near the fort had been used up. Some natives traded large quantities of wood for supplies, hauling most of it to the fort in canoes, travelling further and further away in search of easy gathering.

At 10:30 a.m., the *George S. Wright* steamed into the harbor and weighed anchor. Several Indian canoes paddled toward the ship to ferry goods to the fort. Stanley traded their own canoe for a ride on one of them. Only three canoes returned to the fort with trade items, two with beaver pelts, furs and hides. Fall was not the best time to gather hides due to poor quality, but some had been brought to a trading fort in Alaska earlier than normal because natives still killed animals to eat, and received whatever price they could for the skins. The third canoe was filled with cured caribou meat. The company steamer didn't normally deliver trade goods to the Hudson's Bay Company, but a special request of the caribou meat had been made on the ship's way north. The captain saw a way to make a small profit by delivering the meat and selling the hides and furs he'd traded for, but was quite disappointed with the prices the trading fort offered for the poor quality hides. By 1:00 p.m., the Wright steamed out of the harbour and started southward. In the mess hall that evening,

Stephen was surprised to see his self-proclaimed, whiskey-drinking teacher, Ben, who had been transferred from the *Mumford*. Stephen told him about Jock's murder and what had happened with Evers. He also told him that he'd seen what made the horrible screams on their way north. Ben didn't believe him, laughing at his discription of the Bukwas. Stephen said no more about it and changed the subject.

Over the next four days Stephen and Stanley caught sight of a few whaling ships, one of which they passed within three hundred feet. The whaler had recently made a kill and was in the process of hauling whale blubber on board. The crimson coloured sea water surrounding the ship was a gruesome sight, and both knew they could not be whalers. They also saw several logging operations along the main shore, using steam donkeys to yard the large conifer trees to the water's edge. The steam whistle from the operations reverberated off the mountainside, sounding loud and out of place.

The four days went by quickly as the two men relaxed and chatted frequently with the other few passengers and crewmen. On a late afternoon, the ship pulled into the New Westminster dock.

Finding a room, Stephen and Stan relaxed in hot baths and tipped back a few whiskeys before eating. Stephen ordered the fresh halibut steak and thought it to be the best ocean fish he'd ever eaten. He remembered Mariana had ordered a halibut dinner at the Comstock in San Francisco. She too, had relished the unique taste.

At 9:00 a.m. they entered Conway's office, and Stephen set a small cloth bag by the door. Conway greeted them warmly, smiling, shaking hands with both.

"I'm pleased you're back, Mr. Doyle. I was afraid something happened to you when you didn't show up after that early snow and cold weather. I see you have your map there." Conway nodded toward the rolled oilskin in Stephen's hand. "I'm most anxious to see your results. Let's just roll it out on this map table by the window and see what we have here."

Stephen unwrapped the oilskin while Conway moved several other maps to the side, clearing a spot for it. Conway placed a finger on Stephen's starting point at the bottom of the map, reading his recorded latitude and longitude, comparing it with one he'd written on a sheet of paper. He didn't appear concerned over the slight discrepancy. He moved his finger up the mapped route, reading the short notes to the side, which correlated to specific pages of Stephen's journal—details of creek crossings, timber types and sizes, as well as soils type, especially areas containing bedrock.

Several minutes later, his finger had reached Buck's Bar. Still leaning over the map studiously he said, "Is that your journal you have with you?"

"Yes, sir, it's a lot more descriptive than the map. I was only able to put major details on it." He handed the journal to Conway.

Conway leafed through the journal and then placed a hand on Stephen's shoulder. "Excellent work, Mr. Doyle. You've done an exemplary job with the map. One of the best I've seen come from the bush. I'll be anxious to go through your journal in detail. On the surface, it looks like you've found our best route. So tell me your overall evaluation of the route. Is it workable?"

Stephen felt apprehensive about the question and it reflected in his answer. "Well sir…I tried the best I could to envision the pole line along the route. I made many side trips to gain better vantage points and look for alternate routes when obstacles were evident. Javier Vega told me what to watch for along the proposed route, but fact is, Mr. Conway, I don't know if I'm qualified to give you an answer for sure. My gut feeling though is, yes…I think it's a workable route."

"That's just what I hoped to hear from you, Mr. Doyle," Conway said with a smile. "My experience has been that a man who doesn't know a whole lot about something like this is more apt to be a bit conservative with his answer. If you think it will work, then by cracky, you're more than likely right. It should work! I'll go through your journal right away and relate your comments to the map. I have to finalize a route for startup next spring. We're not going to stop our work yet. That Atlantic cable will probably fail again, and if so, we may just have the last three hundred miles of our needed exploration completed. Now, let's set for a spell and you can tell me what happened to our man, Jock Dubois.

Stephen related the entire incident, and Conway grew incensed as he listened. He agreed that the Atlantic Cable Company might be behind the plot. Stephen asked if he should go to the local constable and report it. Conway said he would take care of it tomorrow, it would be best if Stephen just went on back to San Francisco later that day on the same ship he'd caught from Fort Rupert.

"Those are Jock's personal things in the bag there," Stephen said, pointing toward the door. "I feel obligated to stay a few days and find his wife...tell her what happened to him."

Conway thought for a moment, then said, "No, I'll have someone take care of that, Doyle. I'll send her money for Jock's pay, too, just as if he'd completed the job with you. I think it's best if you just go on home and collect your pay from Mr. Bulkley. I'll wire him today that you'll be arriving on the *Wright* and will stop by with my voucher. I'll tell him about Jock too, and who may have put this Ryan Evers guy up to these murderous tactics. There'll probably be more if they think we're going to successfully get to Europe."

Stephen pondered Conway's take-charge decisions. Having visualized himself telling Jock's wife about his murder and offering to do whatever he could to help, he felt uneasy about someone else telling her. But then, that's Conway's job, to make these quick determinations. Maybe he's right about handling it all.

"Mr. Conway, would you mind sending a message for me when you send one to Mr. Bulkley. It's to my boss, Hugh Randall; let him know when the ship will be pulling in."

"Sure thing, Doyle," Conway said reaching for paper and pen. "Just write it out here and I'll take care of it."

Conway and Mitchell talked while Stephen wrote the message to Hugh. When he finished, he listened for a moment while Mitchell added a few details about their canoe trip down the Skeena.

Conway noticed Stephen had finished the telegram and rose to his feet. "Well, if that's all, Mr. Doyle, just follow me to my bookkeeper's office and well get that voucher filled out for you. Mitchell," he said, turning to Stanley. "Wait here. I'll be just a moment and we'll go over your plans for the winter."

Stephen moved toward Stan with his hand extended and Stan rose from the chair, realizing this would be their final good-bye. Stephen said, "I just wanted you to know, Stanley, that when I first thought about you and me paddling downriver together, I figured I was going to do all the work. You looked a bit puny to me...but you proved me wrong. I'll travel with you anywhere, any time. You're a good hand, Stan, I'm proud to know you."

"The feeling is mutual, Stephen. I mean…I don't mean I thought you were puny. I mean it's been my great pleasure to have travelled in your entertaining company. We certainly showed that Skeena River a thing or two about canoeing." And they both laughed at the thought of inexperienced canoeists tackling one of the largest and most difficult rivers in the north.

Stephen followed Conway to the accountant's office and Conway instructed a $1,500 voucher to be made to Stephen Doyle, credited to, "Route Exploration."

Stephen returned to their room to gather his things and he left Mitchell a note, giving his home and office address, telling him he would be most welcome to stay with him if he ever came to California.

He walked to the Fraser River pier and boarded the *George S. Wright* an hour before departure. He went directly to his cabin and stowed his goods for the four-day trip. Stephen lay on his bunk, reflecting, then went topside a while later. Three short blasts of the ship's steam whistle signified the gangplank being hoisted, and a voice shouted out from the dock below. "Wait…wait just a minute. I'm coming aboard."

He looked down to see Stan Mitchell with his pack, running toward the gangplank. Puzzled, Stephen moved toward the boarding ramp while Stan handed the officer a note from Conway.

"Where the heck you headed for, Stanley? This ship's going to San Francisco you know?"

"I know." Mitchell said, trying to catch his breath. "Conway thought it would be beneficial to the company if I visited the San Francisco office. They might even find some work for me. Thought I might take you up on that offer for a bed."

Surprised at the sudden decision, Stephen said, "Hey, it will be my pleasure, Stanley. Just need to move a few things around when we get there." His thoughts immediately went to Michael's bedroom and what he would have to do. Could he really do it?

Over the next four days, Stephen and Stan got to know each other more intimately. On the way downriver, Stephen had told him about Rachel and Michael disappearing one afternoon. Now, he told him of his inner battle, struggling with thoughts of their reappearance and the battle over his feelings for Mariana.

He hoped to see her again and restore their relationship, but hopefully without guilty feelings when he went home to bed. He'd even considered selling the house and buying another across the city.

Stan Mitchell had never married and now at forty-four, doubted he ever would. Consequently, he had little advice to offer his friend.

When at last they pulled through the Golden Gate and into the large bay, Stephen's excitement heightened upon seeing the numerous buildings of the sprawling city. The thought that kept returning, though, was of walking into that empty house. He dreaded it, and had mixed feelings about Stan being there right away. He had been considering asking Stan if he would mind getting a room close by, until he felt more comfortable about a guest. But on the other hand, perhaps it would be better to just have him move in immediately. He would think on it a little longer.

The two men had their gear on deck and stood peering toward the dock as the ship tied up in the mid-afternoon breeze. Stephen spotted Hugh and shouted out, waving his arm. Being the first down the gangplank, he hurried to where Hugh waited, dropping his pack on the pier deck. Hugh looked at him strangely.

"Are you sure you're the same guy I sent off on a voyage up the coast? You sure do look different with three months of hair on your face." He laughed and threw his arms around Stephen. The two hugged, patting each other on the back, showing their strong affection.

Stanley stood close by, smiling at the reunion. No one waited for him back in Montreal like this, and the thought came that he would probably never go back there. Both parents had passed away and his brother had been killed in a coal mine in northern Ontario the year he came out west to take the new telegrapher job.

Stephen introduced the two men and told Hugh that Stan would be staying with him for a while.

Hugh looked relieved and said, "Yes, that's probably a good idea, Stephen. It'll be good for you to have someone there." He paused while looking into Stephen's eyes, as if he had something else to say. "Come, my horse and wagon are just off the dock around the corner."

Stan insisted on setting in the back of the wagon so the two could talk on the way home."So, what is that north country like?" Hugh asked as if his thoughts were on a different matter.

"*Oh Hugh,* you wouldn't believe that country up there. High mountain peaks with glaciers, and trees everywhere; some almost as big as those redwoods up north. Before snow fell on the peaks, the mountains above timberline were the most beautiful lush green. It just made you want to be up there and stroll through it. Those peaks were so high, I just know that if you were on top of them, you could see clear back to the ocean, over a hundred miles I'd bet."

Stephen rambled nonstop for several minutes before pausing long enough for Hugh to interrupt.

"Stephen," he said turning in the seat to look at him. "I've got something I need to tell you." He paused, thinking of the best way to start. "Something happened while you were gone. It won't be easy for you to hear, but hear it you must."

"What the heck, Hugh," Stephen said, a frown creasing his brow. "My house burn down or something?"

"No...no, not that, Stephen. But it has been cleaned out some."

"You mean someone broke in and stole everything? Oh, for crying out loud! I can't believe..."

"*No,*" Hugh interrupted, then turned to look straight ahead, not seeing anything particular. "Just listen, boy. This is hard enough as it is. Stephen, ...Rachel has come back. She's not at your house. She's at her folks."

Stunned, Stephen's adrenaline surged at the thought. "Are you kidding me, Hugh? You wouldn't BS me on this would you? Rachel *is back*? Are you sure it's her? Did you see her? Michael, what about Michael? Is my boy there too?"

"Slow down, Stephen. I told you this was going to be hard for you. Now just listen, boy. Please...just listen." Stephen sat quietly, but inside, his thoughts raced wildly, waiting to hear the rest, wondering what had happened.

"Rachel and Michael were shanghaied. That's why they disappeared so suddenly. Three men pulled them into an alley and put something on Rachel's face, and she blacked out. She woke up on a ship called the *Blackhawk,* far out to sea. She'd been chained below because she refused to do the work they told her to if she wanted to eat. It was several days before they let her go up for fresh air. She begged them to let her see Michael, but they wouldn't.

They threatened to withhold food from Michael unless she gave in to their demands. She finally did, after hearing Michael crying on the deck right above her.

They were rough on Michael, trying to make him into a cabin boy, and when Rachel finally saw him after 17 days, he was hungry and filthy. She vowed to do whatever they demanded if they would take care of him.

"Her duties were to help in the galley in daytime, and spend nights in the beds of the Captain and his two mates."

"*Oh, no,*" Stephen moaned. "*Oh, God, no, not that! Not my poor Rachel.* Oh geez, Hugh." his voice breaking. Then through clenched teeth he said "How in hell can those sons-a-bitches do that to her? I'll kill the bastards, Hugh. *I'll hunt them down and kill them rotten bastards!*"

"There now, son," Hugh said consolingly, patting his knee. "I know it's hard for you to hear. It was for me too. But you've got to buck up. There's more to tell." Stephen looked at Hugh, and in exasperation, his shoulders slumped and he exhaled loudly, nodding for him to continue.

"Little Michael got sick. Real sick. And they let Rachel care for him some. But it wasn't soon enough. He died on the ship Stephen, a month after they took him. They buried him at sea." Stephen moaned in pain and spoke Michael's name several times. After a long silence, Hugh continued.

"Rachel just gave up after Michael was gone. Quit eating and didn't take care of herself anymore. The men didn't care. Still took their selfish pleasure from her, then kicked her out afterwards. Told her she smelled too bad to be with for long. They stripped her once in a while in front of the crew, then threw water on her while one of the mates washed her down. She didn't care anymore. Never looked at the men. Sort of saw right through them, I guess.

"The ship sailed around the horn and over to Africa. Rachel tried to run away when they docked, but they caught her and chained her again until they left port for Portugal. After that, Greece and Italy, then England. She didn't leave the ship in all that time. They finally took her ashore in England and she tricked them. She got a shopkeeper to let her hide in a backroom, and the shopkeeper told two men from the ship that she'd slipped out the front door and down the street when the were looking the other way. An English ship finally brought her back home. There's a bit more to tell after her escape, but that's enough for now.

"The other hard part for you in all this, Stephen, is Rachel is not the same woman you once knew. She wants nothing to do with men anymore, including you, son. Something happened to her on that trip, the way men treated her and all. Her pa came to my office and told me all this. Thought it best if I'm the one to tell you. She had her folks move all her and Michael's things out of your house. Her pa told me she'd already petitioned for a divorce of your marriage. I went up to see her once, but she wouldn't talk to me. Her folks are just broken hearted about it. They'll probably keep her there in their house until they both die, her pa said. Then she'll just have to figure out what to do. Damn shame. Just a real damn shame and I'm sorry I was the one that had to tell you. But better from me than anyone else."

He put an arm around Stephen and pulled him closer. "You'll be fine, son. You've got a lot of heart. She's been gone from you for a year and a half now. She never came back to you, Stephen. She came back to her ma and pa and you've got to leave it at that. Best thing you can do is go see that little Californio' girl you were getting sweet on."

Stephen felt a hand on his shoulder and looked at Stan standing behind. "I'm sorry, Stephen. That was a hard one for even me to hear. Hugh, if you would just drop me off at a hotel, I think Stephen needs to be by himself tonight."

Stephen placed a hand on top of Stan's and said, "Thanks, pal. It is going to be a difficult night."

They drove Stan to a hotel near the Western Union Extension Company office and Stephen told him he would be by in a couple of days. Hugh drove the wagon to Stephen's house and asked if he wanted him to come in for a while, get a fire going, heat some water, help him adjust. Stephen declined, wanting to be alone. To think things over. Sort things out.

Stephen unlocked the front door, leaving his pack outside. Glancing around the living room, he noticed a few small items were missing: a vase here, a wall painting there. Walking into the kitchen was similar, only a couple of items he could think of were gone. The upper cupboards still held dishes, the lower had cooking pots and pans.

He went to the upstairs bedrooms, knowing this would be the biggest change. He looked in Michael's room first. All his things were gone, except the bed. It had to have been hard for her to go through them, or perhaps her father and mother did that for her. He walked to their bedroom. The bed was made up and there was a note on his pillow. Sitting on the bed, he reached for the folded piece of paper, and read the two handwritten pages:

Dearest Stephen:

I find this letter extremely difficult to write. I could not leave it for others to explain to you, so I know I must do this myself.

I am sure Hugh has told you of the things I have been through, so I will not refer to them, except for Michael. When he died from the high fever, I no longer had a reason to want to live, except for you. But the men took that away from me too. I hated them for what they took from me and what they did to me. It is because of these men that I can never be with you again. I could not be a wife to you or for you. My dignity is gone. My womanhood has been stripped away. They treated me as they would an animal, and I feel my hatred for men can never be extinguished.

I do not hate you, Stephen, but I can no longer love you the way I once did. Because of this, I must set you free to love again. I hope beyond all means that somehow you understand. I will be petitioning for a dissolution of our marriage. Please forgive me.

In memory of the love we once had.
Rachel

Stephen felt the sadness and hurt build inside. Not just for his now certain loss of his precious wife, but for her loss of what had been taken from her and what she felt inside. He lay back on the bed and placed an arm across his forehead. He began swallowing hard, trying to hold back his hurt. Feeling his eyes beginning to water, he slowly closed them. His thoughts went back through what Rachel had said, as tears trickled down the back of his cheeks and into his ears. One of the thoughts was, unless she can eventually overcome the way she feels about men, she will never know love again. But he knew too, and for some reason felt confident that, Rachel would somehow, some way, find the courage to change things and find love in her life again.

Stephen lay on the bed a long time before sitting up. He had made some decisions as he lay, thinking of the past life with Rachel and Michael, of his exploration north and, of his future.

He looked into the empty clothes closet and chest of drawers as a final act of abdication, before walking back down the stairs.

He started a fire to heat water for bathing and brought his pack inside, taking all the smoky-smelling items onto the back porch to air out. While unpacking, he noticed that the only items he had as a remembrance of the trip, outside of a thumb and leg scar, were the bent rifle barrel and the .32 caliber pistol. Both would be an adequate reminder of the circumstances in which they were obtained.

He stripped off his clothes, bathing and shaving his three months of facial hair. He'd never had a beard before and it hurt somewhat to shave. His face felt naked and cold. He saw too, that he badly needed a haircut.

Dressed, he walked out the door and uphill to the nearest diner. A simple meal of thick juicy beef steak, mashed potatoes with extra gravy and creamed carrots were one of the finest he could remember, having dreamed about it for months.

The following morning he visited his old barber, telling him of the three-month absence from the city. The next stop was the gold commissioner's office, where he exchanged the gold he'd found at the prospectors' camp, receiving $325. He reflected upon the shallow grave he'd placed the men's remains in for exchange of the gold. Then, he walked to the Western Union Company office, where he asked for Mr. Charles Bulkley.

"Mr. Doyle," Bulkley said as they sat. "Conway sent me a telegram to let me know you would be coming in. He read through your journal and said you had some remarkable encounters. I would like you to come to our Board meeting next week and tell us all about them. It would be a great insight for those of us stuck in the office end of the company."

"Well…ah, I'm not any good at talking in front of a bunch of people, Mr. Bulkley. I…I don't…"

"Nonsense, boy," Bulkley interrupted. "There are only six, and you won't have any problem talking to us. We're mostly down-to-earth fellows. You'll do just fine. Now, another thing Conway mentioned: your information was some of the best detailed he's seen and that you have found us the route we'll take. He recommended you for a bonus. So if you will give me your voucher, I'll take it out front and return with your well-earned money."

When Bulkley returned, he counted out $1,500 in cash and another $300 as a bonus, more money than Stephen had ever seen at one time.

"I would like to hear of some of your adventures right now, Mr. Doyle, but I'll refrain from asking until I can hear all of it next week," he said, walking Stephen toward the door. "I'll send you a letter giving the day and time of our meeting."

Stephen shook Bulkley's hand and thanked him for the opportunity to be of service to the company. Bulkley told him they just may require his services again.

Stephen walked away with a little extra spring in his step, going directly to his bank near Hugh's office, depositing most of the money from the gold and payment for his services. He then stopped at an agency which helped people buy and sell homes, putting his house up for sale, then went straight to Hugh's office.

Hugh sat at his desk, looking up as the door opened. "*Well, Stephen.* I wasn't sure if I would see you today. How are you son? Sit down and we'll talk," he said, nodding toward the chair across from his desk. "Are you okay?"

"Yeah, Hugh. I'm good. Rachel left a letter for me on our bed. She explained her feelings and why she became hardened the way she is. After I thought about it a while, how it must have been for her on that ship, Michael dying, and those men treating her like they would a damn dog, I understood. I'm just glad she's alive...she can still get back to normal, you know. At least, I'm hoping she can. It hurts, Hugh. It really hurts."

"I know it does, Stephen. But you'll eventually get through it. It'll just take some time. At least you're not going to be wondering if she'll suddenly show up someday. You can move on with your life now, lad ...right?"

"Yes, that's just what I've decided to do, Hugh. I've been paid for the telegraph survey and I'm going to sell my house. I'm taking a little time off, if it's all right with you: do a little travelling—relax a bit before I put my nose to the grindstone."

Hugh nodded slowly while reflecting on Stephen's sudden decision to sell his house, then take off for..."Where were you thinking of travelling to?"

"Oh, I was considering a boat trip around Cape Horn and up to New York, then back across country by train and horse. I rather liked the ocean, and I'd like to take a sailing clipper. I heard on the ship ride back home that they can make it to New York in three months now. Another couple of months to get back here, and I'll be ready for work in late spring or so."

"Well," Hugh said, somewhat disappointed, "Sounds like you've got it all figured out. I'm not going to tell you it's a bad idea. Maybe it's a good idea under the circumstances. Now, tell me about your trip up north."

Stephen talked for two hours, telling everything that had happened and what the country was like, all the way from San Francisco to Buck's Bar. He showed Hugh the scar on his leg from the wolf bite and the split thumb that grew back a little fatter on one side. He described the Bukwas in great detail and Hugh shook his head trying to imagine it all. Stephen also told him why he would not tell the Bukwas stories to very many people, as Kwabellum instilled in him fear of the white men coming to kill or capture the giant creature.

Stephen talked until early afternoon. Upon leaving, he left money with Hugh to take to Rachel. Before going to Mariana Vega's home, he hired a single horse buggy to take him to the harbor docks, asking the driver to wait at each stop. He talked to three ship captains, five saloon keepers, six dock warehouse foremen, and the harbor master.

The two questions he asked were: "Have you heard of a ship called the *Blackhawk*?" and, "Where can I find it?"

EPILOGUE

GENERALLY CALLED "BUKWAS" OR "BOQS" WITHIN THE DIFFERENT languages along the coast of British Columbia, another frequently used Indian word meaning "Hairy Giant" or "Wild Man of the Woods", is known today as "Sasquatch." "Bigfoot" is also a common name used for the huge, apelike creature that reportedly roams the forested mountains. It has been the source of legends for centuries throughout the tribes and bands of Indians all along the West Coast of the United States and Canada.

This legendary creature is alleged to have a thick covering of one-inch long hair ranging in colour from grey or light brown to black, with glossy reddish-brown, commonly reported. Some reports claim the hair covers the entire body, including the face. Others say the mouth, nose, ears and palm of the hands are barren of hair. The giant stands between seven and nine-feet tall and weighs 600 to 900 pounds. Its arms are long, hanging below the knees, and the arms swing to and fro like a human's when it walks at a fast pace. A Bukwas moves about on two massive legs with strides similar to man, except theirs is twice the length of an average person. The footprints are similar to that of humans', but the giant's print averages sixteen inches in length and six in width, compared to ten inches and four in width on a man, and the toes are more squared at the front than a human's. Taking into account these distinguishing features, is the creature a humanoid or is it an animal? Perhaps part of both.

At times, the powerful creature depicts a gentle disposition and perhaps a hint of compassion, according to the account of an abducted man named Albert Ostman in 1924, who implies that the creatures are people. On the other hand, they can be ferocious when angered or provoked, as reported by several different individuals. Bukwas's have chased people, violently shaken automobiles while the passengers screamed inside, killed and torn apart a man, and in a separate incident broke a man's neck. They have killed and eaten domestic animals and are believed by some Indians of the northern Yukon Territory to have eaten human flesh. They have been shot point blank and ran away.

These giants step over four-foot high fences without breaking stride, walk up steep roadside cuts with ease and slip quietly into the brush, disappearing as suddenly as they appear. They have been heard vocalizing screams, shrieks, howls, whistles, hoots and grunts, most of which sound like no other animal on earth. Many accounts of differing peculiarities abound throughout written records of numerous interviews conducted by authors of several published books.

Does the Bukwas truly exist? Those who claim to have seen a "hairy giant" certainly believe it. Many think it could be possible. Most say it is not possible, where is the evidence? An amateur film exists of a probable female Bukwas, which some scientists shrug off without explanation. Other men of science say the film is not a fake, but will say no more about it.

Outside of many plaster casts of footprints from many parts of the continent, where is further evidence? Perhaps it is contained in the large rocks dug out of a hole and piled neatly to the side in pursuit of a rock rabbit or pika, or bent oil drums that had been tossed down a hillside, both incidents blamed on a Bukwas. But is it proof? No skeletal remains have ever been found. But then how many have ever seen, in the wild, the skeletal remains of a bear, or mountain lion that has died of natural causes? Until April, 2001, no specimen of this mysterious creature had been supplied to the scientific world. Bryan Sykes, Professor of Human Genetics at the Institute of Molecular Medicine in Oxford, England analyzed the DNA from a hair sample of a reported Yeti in Bhutan. He said this, "We've never encountered DNA that we couldn't recognize before. We don't know what it is — but then, we weren't looking for the Yeti."

Science continually proves that it is possible for a previously undiscovered creature to exist in the world. Perhaps someday someone will capture or kill a Bukwas specimen for science to ponder and catagorize. If so, a new species will have been born, yet, one that has existed for hundreds of years. Perhaps even thousands.

Likely you are one who says adamantly, "I will believe it when I see it!"

An account of Albert Ostman's story can be found in, *On the Track of the Sasquatch,* by John Green.

Other mentioned incidents can be found in *Encounters With Bigfoot,* by John Green, *Sasquatch: Bigfoot, The Continuing Mystery,* by Thomas N. Steenburg,

Grizzlies & White Guys, by Harvey Thommasen, *Science Looks at Mysterious Monsters,* by Thomas G. Aylesworth and David Thompson's diary, page 64, BC Archives.

The 1967 amateur film of a female Sasquatch taken by Roger Patterson, is occasionally shown on various television programs. An account of the incident can be read in John Green's, *On the Track of the Sasquatch.*

ENDNOTES

[1]**Gitanmaax:** People who fish by torchlight.

[2]**Kuldo Village:** Galdo'o, or, back woods.

[3]**Wa Dzun Kwuh River, in Wet'suwet'en language:** a canyon.

In Gitxsan language the same river is called: Xs'an An'doo'o, or, on the other side.

[4]**Skeena River, in Gitxsan language:** Xsii 'yeen, or river of mists.

[5]**Nass River:** Xsitxemsem, or, food basket.

[6]**Stikine River, a Tahltan name:** Stikine, or, muddy water.

[7]**Gitxsan:** People of the river of mists.

[8]**Hagwilget, in Wet'suwet'en language:** Tse-kya, or, base of rock.

In Gitxsan language: Place of the quiet people.

[9]**Wet'suwet'en:** People of the lower valley

[10]**Kitsagas Village:** Kisgaga'as, or, people of the place with the small white gull.

[11]**Klappan River, a Tahltan name:** Hla bonna, or, all goodness without badness.

[12]Unknown to the Western Union Extension Company, the race was over. The Atlantic Cable worked perfectly. The Western Union Extension Company did not concede defeat until the following year.

BIBLIOGRAPHY

Gitxsan Treaty Office, Tribal Boundaries in the Nass Watershed

Rosemary Neering, *Continental Dash – The Russian-American Telegraph*

Norma V. Bennett, *Pioneer Legacy – Chronicles of the Lower Skeena, Volume 1*

Dr. Robert Galois, *(The Spirit of the Land) The History of the Upper Skeena Region 1850-1927*

Guy Lawrence, *40 Years on the Yukon Telegraph*

Ken Campbell, *Fort Simpson, Fur Fort at Laxtgu'Alaams*

Howard White, *Metlakatla – Peoples of Canada*

P.J. Leech, *The Pioneer Telegraph Survey of British Columbia*

A.L. Poudrier, *Report of Crown Land Surveys – Exploration Survey of New Caledonia*

Encyclopedia of the American West, Simon & Schuster, 1996

Colliers Encyclopedia, Macmillan Educational Co., 1989

Daniel Cohen, *Everything You Need to Know About Monsters and Still Be Able to Get to Sleep,* 1989

Peter Byrne, *The Search For Bigfoot: Monster, Myth or Man*

David George Gordon, *Field Guide to Sasquatch*

CMI 063

#243